There's a fine line
between right and wrong.

MISTER
WRONG

NICOLE
new york times bestselling author
WILLIAMS

Mister Wrong
Copyright © 2017
Nicole Williams

ISBN-13: 978-1-940448-15-2 | ISBN-10: 1-940448-15-8

Without limiting the rights under copyright reserved above, no part of this publication may be reproduced, stored in or introduced into a retrieval system, or transmitted, in any form, or by any means (electronic, mechanical, photocopying, recording, or otherwise) without the prior written permission of the copyright owner of this book, except by a reviewer who may quote brief passages for review purposes

This is a work of fiction. Names, characters, places, brands, media, and incidents either are the product of the author's imagination or are used fictitiously. The author acknowledges the trademarked status and trademark owners of various products referenced in this work of fiction, which have been used without permission. The publication/use of these trademarks is not authorized, associated with, or sponsored by the trademark owners.

All rights reserved.

Dedicated to everyone who's met the right person at the wrong time.

CHAPTER ONE

Matt

He was wrong for her.

That was the only thought running through my head as I rechecked every inch of the church. So completely wrong for her. This latest disappearing act, the most recent proof. He'd skipped out on her before, but today was different.

Today, they were supposed to get married. Today, Cora Matthews would become Cora Adams. She'd have my last name. But not in the way I'd hoped for—not that I hadn't accepted that years ago.

She'd chosen him. My brother. My *twin* brother. She'd chosen him forever ago, and that was that. She'd been as good as Mrs. *Jacob* Adams since the day Cora Matthews first showed up in our lives years ago.

At least until today, when Cora was going to be marching toward an empty altar in fifteen minutes if I didn't find the supposed Mister Right. Jacob wasn't the right one—for a dozen reasons I could list—but he was who she wanted and he'd done his best to convince her she was all he wanted too. But I knew better.

My brother had always been indulged; being the "firstborn" son—by a whole three minutes—to a wealthy family has a way of doing that. The problem arose when the boy grew into a man who wanted to be equally indulged in all sorts of ways that a wife would likely frown upon. Jacob wasn't the right one for her. I knew that. Hell, I think even he knew that when he surfaced from his self-adoring stupor every so often.

Not that I was the right one for Cora either. I was just as wrong for her as Jacob was, but in a different way. See, where he'd always loved her too little, I'd loved her too much. So I'd kept my secret for years and watched the girl I loved fall in love with the brother I'd shared a womb with for thirty-eight weeks. The brother I loved and looked after, despite his faults.

God knew I had a shit ton of my own.

That was why I was about to start tearing this church apart in order to find him. I was looking after his interests as well as Cora's, because even though he had a piss-poor way of showing it, he loved her. In his own way. If you could call what Jacob felt for anyone love. In a way, it was love, but in another way, it was the opposite.

"Where the hell's Jacob?" The senior Adams, also known as Dad, asked when I circled into the lobby again, hoping my missing brother had magically appeared. He was holding my brother's tux zipped up in an expensive bag and looking at me like I was failing the task of keeping track of my brother as I'd failed all the rest presented to me in life.

Where the hell's Jacob? How many times had I asked myself that question? How many times had I probably known or had a good idea where he was?

"He's back in one of the church offices waiting. Just got here." I had to slow myself down when I heard the words wobble. It had been years since I'd stuttered over a word, and now was not the time to resurrect that old habit. "I'll take it down to him."

I grabbed the tux from Dad and backed down the hall, trying to ignore the stuffed sanctuary and the orchestra playing some song that sounded more fitting for a funeral than a wedding.

That was what this was about to become if I didn't do something. Whether it would be my dad murdering me for flunking my best man responsibilities of keeping track of the groom, or me murdering Jacob when I finally found his pathetic ass after doing this to Cora on today of all days, someone was going to die.

"That tux isn't going to put itself on a groom, Matt. Get after it." Dad motioned me down the hall before he marched toward the sanctuary like he was ready to get this over with.

He wasn't thrilled about the wedding. Didn't exactly approve of the match. It wasn't that he didn't love Cora, because he did, like a daughter. He just didn't find her fitting as a daughter-in-law, especially to his prized firstborn who was incapable of doing wrong. He probably wouldn't have cared so much if she was marrying me, which was disconcerting to say the least. The *only* person who'd approve of Cora and me ending up together was my dad.

As I jogged down the hall, carrying a found tux to a missing groom, Dad's last words replayed through my mind. *That tux isn't going to put itself on a groom.*

A groom.
A groom.

My plan was already forming as I ducked into a dark church office, my fingers working my tie loose. Jacob wasn't just my twin brother—he was my *identical* twin brother.

I was maybe a little bit taller and he was maybe a little bit fuller, but not enough that anyone would notice. Not enough, I hoped, that Cora would notice. She used to confuse us all the time when we were growing up together and still, on occasion, she'd mistake me for Jacob and Jacob for me. Like the last time I'd been at her and Jacob's condo when she'd thrown a surprise party for him. I'd been talking with a group of old friends, she slid by me, found my hand, and gave it the briefest of squeezes. She'd thought I was Jacob. I knew that because she never touched me anymore. At least not on purpose. We used to be comfortable enough with each other that she'd hug me without thinking, but that changed when she and Jacob became a thing. An official thing.

She didn't touch me anymore, not even to nudge me for saying something stupid, which I said all too often in her presence. But that night, she'd touched me. And a year later, I could still remember the way her small hand felt falling into mine.

Cora would be distracted today—nervous. I knew because she'd told me how panicked she was about standing in front of five hundred people. She'd be so distracted by trying to keep herself from passing out or hyperventilating, so would she really notice if the man standing across from her in front of that altar was me?

I was banking on the chance that she wouldn't, as I changed from my suit into Jacob's tux as fast as humanly possible. The clock on the wall was fast, hopefully, or else I had two and a half minutes to get my ass up front so that when Cora started down the aisle, she'd have someone waiting for her.

Someone who loved her.

As I tied the shiny dress shoes, I tried to put aside all of the inner voices telling me how wrong this was. How utterly and unforgivably wrong this was. I knew it was wrong. I *knew* that. But it was just as wrong to do nothing. It was wrong to let Jacob ruin another moment for her. By doing something that I knew was wrong, I hoped I was ultimately doing the right thing.

Maybe he wasn't where I thought he was, hungover and waking up in some girl's bed. Maybe he'd gotten into an accident or been kidnapped or . . . damn, then I'd feel like a real piece of shit for thinking the worst about my own brother. Maybe something legitimate had come up and he'd have some great explanation and I'd pull him aside to let him know I'd stepped in and no one besides us would know what had gone down.

And maybe Jacob had decided to turn over a new leaf and not be such a selfish prick, I thought with a sigh.

Pausing in front of the picture hanging beside the door, I adjusted the bowtie as best I could before tearing the door open and jogging down the hall. Jacob's tux was a little big for me, and his shoes a little small, but those were minor discomforts compared to what my psyche was putting me through.

The ring.

Fuck.

After sprinting back to the office, I wrestled the ring box out of the pocket of my jacket, along with my wallet and phone—just in case I didn't make it back here anytime soon—then I kicked my suit behind a bookcase in the event that someone stumbled into the room to find an abandoned suit and started asking questions.

My dad's face was red by the time I made it inside the sanctuary, but when he saw me, his face relaxed and he smiled. It took me a moment to realize he wasn't smiling at me—he was smiling at Jacob.

Dad never really smiled at me too much. Smirks were more the way of it.

"Where the hell's Matt?" one of the groomsmen, Hunter, whispered when I passed.

God, this church was stuffed to capacity. And hot. And lacking in oxygen.

"Barfing up his guts," I answered quietly, reminding myself that I was Jacob and needed to talk and sound like him.

The groomsmen rocked with silent laughter. They were all Jacob's friends; none were mine.

"Go figure. We're the ones drinking places dry, and it's your brother, the DD, yacking his insides out today."

My shoulder lifted in the dismissive way Jacob's did. "Some guys have all the luck."

"And some guys named Matt Adams have none," Aaron, another groomsman, whispered up the line.

Didn't I know it?

They didn't make any more jokes or jeers at my expense because they knew better. Jacob and I might have seen things differently and been as unalike as two people could be, but we were twins. He stood up for me and vice versa. He had my back, I had his.

As my current predicament proved.

The orchestra broke into a new song—the "Wedding March". The collar of Jacob's dress shirt felt like it was strangling me at the same time it felt like someone had just dialed up the temperature in the room by twenty degrees.

What am I doing? Why am I doing it? Is it right? Or wrong?

The answers to those questions didn't have a chance to form because that was when I saw her. Like the thousands of times before, the world faded away when Cora Matthews walked into the room. When she started down the aisle, I swayed a little and had to step out of line to keep myself from toppling into the minister.

"Easy there, big guy," Hunter said under his breath, elbowing me. "Too late for cold feet. Bride is en route."

I wanted to tell him it wasn't cold feet I had, but something else. It was the feeling of being so sure of something that the rest of the world seemed off-kilter. So sure of something that the rest of the world just didn't make sense. I'd never been as certain of anything as I was about the woman walking toward me, about to marry me.

Under false pretenses.

I had to remind myself of that when Cora's eyes found mine and her plastered-on smile crumbled behind a real one. She was smiling at me the way she smiled at him—like I was her world.

Matthew Adams had never been her whole world, but unknown to her, she'd been mine. That was why I was standing here now, posing as my twin brother, as his fiancée took the final steps toward me. I was doing this for her because I knew she loved him, and I didn't want to see her hurt again at my brother's hand.

Marry the woman you love, Matt, then let her spend the rest of her life with the man she loves.

The orchestra was just playing its final chords when Cora stopped beside me, her eyes matching the real smile still on her face. God, she was beautiful.

Too beautiful, I thought again, as I noticed the line of groomsmen appraising her with more than just casual regard. Cora had always been more than another one of the pretty girls; she was the standout. Every guy knew the type. The girl who shouldn't be real, but there she was, passing you in the hallway every morning. The girl who's noticed by every person she passes, male or female. She was so beautiful on the outside, few people took the time to get to know the beauty hiding underneath, but I had. I knew she was beautiful everywhere.

Jacob. Channel Jacob, I reminded myself as everyone took a collective seat behind us.

"Hey," I whispered to her, winking.

Hey? What a moron. Who says hey to the woman he's about to marry when she stopped beside him looking so damn perfect. I couldn't feel my lungs.

"Hey," she whispered back, like she didn't think anything of it.

Because, yeah, Jacob totally would have said hey to his bride like a moron.

Cora had been versed in moron for practically two decades.

As the minister started droning on about something I probably should have been paying attention to, I tuned out. This wasn't my wedding. This was hers. This was *his*. So instead I watched Cora, memorizing every detail of her face as she stared at the man across from her, who loved her like she was both a poison and an antidote.

When the pastor asked if I promised to love and cherish her, in sickness and in health, until death do us part, that was the easiest question I'd ever had to answer. It was the simplest part of this mess of a day.

"I will."

CHAPTER TWO

Matt

I was a married man. I'd married the woman I'd loved since we were eight years old.

Then why was my mood so damn grim? I splashed some more cold water onto my face at the sink of one of the many first floor bathrooms inside the house I'd grown up in. Outside, the reception was well under way. I could hear music and celebration spilling across the estate. Why did I feel like I'd soaked my world in kerosene and was about to drop a match?

The wedding had gone fast. Too fast. It felt like five minutes after I'd slipped into Jacob's tux, Cora and I were being announced as husband and wife. If she suspected anything, she hadn't shown it. She'd just said her vows, slipped a ring on my finger, and we'd exchanged an innocent kiss that didn't make me feel innocent things.

I could still feel her lips on mine, the warmth of them seeping into mine, the slightest hint of mint on her breath.

After nearly two decades of fanaticizing about kissing her, I finally had. At her and my brother's wedding. How was that for a story to one day tell the grandkids?

Provided I had any since, yeah, Cora. I'd been so hung up on her, I'd gone on a pathetic handful of dates in my twenty-seven years, and after that kiss . . . fuck, I knew I'd spend the future just as hung up on her.

After drying off my face, I pulled my phone out of my pocket to try calling Jacob again. I'd been sneaking off to the bathroom all night to try to get a hold of him, and this call, like the ones before, ended in the same result. No answer. I was starting to worry. My brother had always drunk more than he should have, which had gotten him into plenty of shady situations.

Usually those situations involved waking up next to some woman whose name he didn't know, but it was past six o'clock. His drunken stupor from last night should have worn off by now, along with the hangover, leaving enough room in his head for realization to hit that, holy shit, today was his wedding day.

Either Jacob hadn't hit pause on whatever party he'd disappeared to last night, or something bad had happened. And I would feel like a real prick if I'd spent the afternoon marrying his fiancée and dancing with her and touching her if he was in some ditch in need of help.

I was just looking up the numbers to some of the local hospitals to see if a Jacob Adams had been admitted when a pounding sounded on the door.

"The ol' ball and chain's looking for you, Adams." Some muffled laughter and more pounding. "That didn't take long. Hopefully she doesn't start sporting mom jeans and cancelling her waxing appointments. Make sure she doesn't let herself go just because she's landed you."

More laughter, followed by a few more comments that had me gripping the edge of the sink. That these friends thought it was okay to say what they did to Jacob about Cora made me see red.

Growing up, I'd heard plenty of lewd locker-room talk about Cora. Most of it derived from the fact that she was pretty much every straight guy's type—though no one could seem to get through to her—but some of it was said because she didn't come from our world. The world of the supposed "elite," where money decided how important you were and were not.

Cora's mom became our nanny after our mom died since Dad knew his way around kids as much as he did a kitchen. Mrs. Matthews was our nanny from the time Jacob and I were eight to the time she lost her fight with breast cancer seven years later. Her daughter, Cora, had grown up right along with us, from sitting at the breakfast table every morning to roaming our school halls.

Even though our dad paid for her to go to the same private schools Jacob and I did, everyone knew she was the daughter of the "hired help." They treated her as less than, and the boys talked about her and viewed her in ways they didn't the girls who came from "good" families.

After she and Jacob finally made their relationship official after graduation, some of the stigma and comments eased off of her, but only some. Here we all were, years later, and the same douchebags from high school were talking about her like she was an inanimate object they could use for their every whim and pleasure.

"Adams, open up already. I need to take a piss and the other bathrooms are occu-piedo." That was Hunter. Drunk Hunter. I'd had just as much experience with drunk Hunter as I had sober Hunter.

When I threw open the door, I fought the urge, as I had hundreds of times before, to wrap my hands around all of their necks. "Cora's my wife, shithead. Show a little respect before I force it out of you."

Okay, not exactly strangling. But not exactly ignoring and moving on.

Hunter grinned like I was making a joke and smacked Preston on the back. "Oh, believe me, man, I respect your wife. Serious, serious respect for a creature that fine."

More laughter. The stench coming off of them was staggering. The reception had only been going for a couple of hours, but they smelled like they'd taken a bath in whiskey.

Biting my tongue, I shoved through my groomsmen. Aaron was holding out a flask for me, but I ignored it. I'd already had a couple glasses of champagne during dinner and the toasts, and my head was feeling fuzzy. Probably more from the situation I'd put myself in than from the alcohol, but still, I was a smarter man than my brother when it came to knowing alcohol limits.

"Dude, talk about cutting it close today with Tits McGee from last night." Preston rung his arm behind my neck as Hunter started taking a piss in the bathroom without closing the door. "You really milked the last moments of your bachelorhood dry."

Hunter staggered in front of the toilet and had to brace himself against the wall. "You're an example for us all, Adams."

My feet froze to the tile. "What in the hell are you talking about?"

"Last night. That chick you hooked up with at the last club we crawled our drunk asses into." Hunter zipped himself back up and staggered out of the bathroom. "When you weren't at the church when you were supposed to be, I figured you must have changed your mind about matrimony."

"I was with another woman last night?" My throat was burning, because I knew it was true. Jacob wasn't in trouble somewhere, in need of my help. Jacob was drunk off his ass, getting a piece of ass that didn't belong to the woman he'd promised to marry.

If he were standing in front of me right now, I would have killed him. Or I would have come close.

"How wasted were you?" Preston whacked my back a few times, shaking his head. "Yes, you left with a woman last night. You said not to tell anyone and that you'd see us at the wedding today."

Outside, I could just make out Cora scanning the party like she was looking for someone. I guessed that someone was me, her husband who'd spent the last fifteen minutes splashing cold water on his face and being reminded of why his brother was so undeserving of the woman who'd promised to be forever faithful to him today.

"Why don't you guys do me a favor and just high-five each other in the face with a chair?" I lifted my middle finger at them as I headed outside. "I've got a honeymoon to get to."

They went with their typical response to everything—laughter. As much as I despised them, they'd been useful for one thing. Now I knew. Jacob was fine. He'd missed his wedding because he'd been drunk-fucking some other woman and I wasn't going to waste another minute worrying about him.

He had some serious explaining to do whenever he surfaced. *He wasn't the only one.* That sent me reaching for another glass of champagne as I headed toward Cora. He'd messed up. So had I.

Would it have been better to just be honest and let her find out what kind of person Jacob really was? Would heartbreak and humiliation have been better than this—marrying the wrong guy as a stand-in for another wrong guy? God, did two wrongs make a right?

My head was spinning, so I drained the champagne in one drink.

"There you are." She reached for me as soon as she saw me coming.

Setting the empty glass on a table, I wound my hand around hers.

"I was starting to worry you were a runaway groom." She was smiling, making a joke, but she had no idea the truth of it.

My fingers tied through hers, and I pulled her closer. My other hand easily found its way around her waist, as if I'd done it a million times before. The reality was entirely different from my fantasy though.

"I'm not going anywhere," I said. "Now, dance with me one more time before I drag you out of here."

Her arms wound around me, her hands tying behind my neck. I'd never felt anything as perfect as having Cora's body pressed against mine, her arms holding me close.

"Someone a little excited for the honeymoon?" The little uptick in her voice toward the end alluded to what she was getting at.

And shit. I was getting hard. Hearing her hint, imagining her body pinned below mine . . .

She must have felt it, because she pressed a little closer, lifting her mouth to my ear. "Now you've got me all excited too."

My body trembled against hers while I clamped my eyes closed and tried to erase the image of me moving above her from my mind. She was Jacob's, I reminded myself. No matter the mistakes he'd made or how he'd betrayed her, when she touched me and whispered things into my ear, she was talking to Jacob. Not me.

"Come on." Her lips brushed the side of my neck. "Let's get out of here."

When her face came around in front of mine again, there was something in her eyes. It almost looked like confusion, but it passed a moment later.

Might have had something to do with the cologne I wore not being anything like the one Jacob did.

Taking her hand, I steered us through a crowd of people who were intent upon slowing us down to shower us with more congratulations and marital advice. I wasn't sure how never going to bed angry was supposed to be the end-all for a successful marriage, but what the hell did I know?

We'd almost made it inside when I felt a hand clamp over my shoulder. It was a familiar hand touching me in an unfamiliar way. Like I was the golden child. Instead of the tarnished one.

"Hell of a night, son. I'm happy for you." Dad had a tumbler of scotch in his other hand, looking at me like I was everything he could ever hope for in a son. "I'm happy for you both." He leaned in to give Cora a quick peck on the cheek, and she responded with a hug.

My dad had never been overly warm with Cora despite the years she'd spent under his roof, but he'd never been cold either. He'd held her at a careful distance, kind of like the way he held me.

Jacob was the only one allowed past that arm's length distance.

"Thanks, Dad," I said. "This was one hell of a day for sure."

He gave my shoulder one more squeeze before tipping his head inside the house. "Now get out of here and enjoy your honeymoon."

Cora smiled, the faintest color bleeding into her cheeks. "Thank you for such a nice wedding, Mr. Adams."

Dad lifted his drink. "Thank you for taking such good care of my son."

He'd disappeared into the crowd by the time we stepped inside. Dad owned a big commercial real estate company and knew, or was known by, most everyone in Miami's upper circle. That was the reason for the garishly large wedding. I knew Cora would have preferred to keep it a small, quiet affair. Like myself, she didn't know most of the people out there toasting to her marriage and happiness. Jacob might have since he and my dad worked together, but he'd gone and missed his own wedding, so most of those guests were here because of my dad —and for the imposter Jacob Adams.

"You have everything packed and ready?" I asked, tugging on the bowtie that had been strangling me like a noose all day.

Cora nodded, climbing the stairs with me, her hand secured in mine. "All I need to do is change and we're out of here."

I still didn't know what I was about to do. Jacob was still missing, and he was supposed to head to an airport and jump on a plane with his wife to go on their ten day honeymoon on St. Thomas. If I told her now what I'd done, she'd be pissed. Like, throw me over the bannister before firing her heels at my smashed body pissed. Cora might have been an angel most of the time, but don't get in her way when she's upset. I knew from personal experience.

But I couldn't just go on her honeymoon and hope she wouldn't figure out what I'd done and who I was. I couldn't just share her honeymoon—and all that came with such an important event—with her. If I did, it wouldn't just be Cora who would kill me once everything came to light—Jacob would too. I'd kill him if our roles had been reversed.

God, it was an impossible situation, and I was starting to doubt my whole plan to act as stand-in groom earlier. I was in too deep to 'fess up now. Admitting the truth would ruin this whole day more than it probably would have been ruined if I'd just told her earlier that Jacob had left her standing at the altar.

"Could you help with my zipper?" Cora paused outside the door of the guest room she must have been staying in, sliding her hair over her shoulder and turning her back to me.

My fingers forgot how to move.

"Jacob?" Her head titled over her shoulder, waiting.

Nothing like hearing her say his name the way I'd always dreamed of hearing her speak mine to break me out of my temporary stupor.

"Yeah, sure." I cleared my throat and focused on the zipper. Instead of what was behind the zipper. And how warm and soft and . . . *focus*. "No problem."

Once I'd lowered the zipper to the middle of her back, I stopped. There was no way I was lowering it any farther because I wasn't sure I could restrain myself if I did. I didn't trust myself.

Cora gave me an amused look when she felt how far, or *not* far, I'd taken her zipper. "You're not getting all chaste on me now that we're married, are you?"

I answered her with a tipped smile, like I guessed Jacob would have, trying to ignore the ache tempting me to shove her up against the wall and prove to her just how not chaste I felt right now.

It seemed to satisfy her. "Good. Because I packed the wrong lingerie if that's the kind of honeymoon you had in mind." She left me with a smile that suggested everything I was already imagining, stepping inside the room and closing the door.

My head fell into the wall. Great. Just fucking great.

Cora was presently getting naked inside that room, one closed door away, ready to leave on her honeymoon with me and a suitcase full of filthy lingerie. I wasn't sure if I was in some kind of temporary heaven or an eternal purgatory, but I was trapped somewhere between a dream and a nightmare.

How could my brother not see what he had? How could he feel anything but unworthy and grateful for the woman who loved him and had just promised to spend forever with him? Did he think he could do better? Did he think anyone could do better than Cora Matthews?!

Realizing what my brother had and how he took her for granted flooded my veins with anger. Rage flooded my system until I found myself storming to Jacob's old room, shoving inside it, and tearing out of his tux. His suitcases were already here and packed, no doubt thanks to Cora. His dress shirt, slacks, and shoes were all laid out, passports and reservation information neatly arranged on the nearby table.

He had it all. He had everything. He had *her*. And he treated it as though it were nothing. Like it was replaceable—a guarantee he could take for granted.

I didn't realize I'd changed into the shirt and slacks until I was tying on the shoes. I still wasn't sure what I was going to do or how I was going to tell her the truth, but I was done letting my head take the lead on this. It had gotten me into this whole mess, so I was turning over what came next in my gut. This felt right, so I was going with it.

Dressing in my brother's clothes, grabbing my brother's honeymoon information, and heading down the hallway with his suitcase in hand toward his wife's room felt right. It wouldn't have felt right if I'd let my head continue to steer me, but fuck that. This felt right in my core, deep inside, and I was going with it.

Cora opened her door right as I came to a stop outside it. She'd changed into a strapless white summer dress, which managed to take my lungs out of commission in the same way her wedding gown had earlier.

"You look . . ." I fumbled for the right word, running my eyes over her the way I was prohibiting my hands from doing.

"Jacob Adams speechless?" She did a little spin, making the hem of her dress float into the air. "I never thought I'd live to see the day."

My arm wound around her waist, incapable of heeding my warnings to look and not touch. I pulled her toward me until her body was fitted as tight against mine as I could get it. "I can't breathe around you, Cora." My forehead creased when her mouth parted. "Let alone form words."

She stared at me for a moment, then her hand molded around the side of my neck. "Thank you."

"For what?" My eyes dropped to her mouth. *Control yourself.* Although I supposed it was a little late for that.

"You promised me that you'd work on some things if we got married." She bit her lip. "And you have. Thank you for that."

My heart broke a little more right then. Because she was wrong. Jacob hadn't changed any—or maybe he had, but for the worse. She'd always held this blind faith in my brother, and it had been for nothing. Because he'd betrayed her. Again, and again, and now on their wedding day.

She was waiting. And I was a fool.

So I kissed her forehead and dropped my head beside hers. "You deserve more than ten times the man I am. The least I can do is make a few improvements to this unfit one." After holding her close for one more moment, I wrangled both of our suitcases into my hands and followed her down the stairs.

"Should we say good-bye to everyone first or . . ." Cora looked hesitantly out at the back lawn swarmed with people.

"Or let's get out of here before anyone sees us."

I'd already pulled the front door open and was waiting for her. Cora didn't like crowds or big affairs. That had been one of our few common bonds growing up. So when Jacob would sneak off to whatever party was the biggest and best that weekend, we'd hang behind and order cheese pizza and watch movies until we both passed out on the couch.

She beamed as she rushed through the door, taking light steps so her heels wouldn't make any noise in the marble foyer. The house I'd grown up in was closer to the size of a hotel than the average house, and maybe that was why it had never felt like home. Nowhere had ever really felt like home actually, not even the condo I'd been in for several years.

The driver who had escorted us from the church back to the house for the reception was waiting out front to take us to the airport. When he saw us rushing away from the house, he folded up his newspaper and reached for one of the suitcases in my hands.

"Little excited for the honeymoon?" He gave me a knowing look as I tucked Cora's bag into the trunk beside mine.

I answered with a reserved smile because, yes, had Cora been my actual wife and I was the husband she'd planned on marrying today, I would have thrown her over my shoulder and left as soon as the cake had been cut. But she wasn't my actual wife and I wasn't the husband she'd planned on marrying today so what was there to look forward to? Because I couldn't . . . we couldn't . . . I couldn't let her . . . without confessing . . . *fuck, I was in such a bad spot.*

After I slid into the seat beside her, the driver closed the door.

"Buckle up," she said, already winding the belt around my lap.

A better man might have taken the belt from her and clicked it into place himself. I think I'd already proven that I was not that better man.

"We're in a limousine. Don't think we need to worry about buckling up."

She blew out a breath after she'd snapped the buckle into place. "And limousines can still get in accidents. I'd like my husband in good working order for our honeymoon, please." Her hand dropped to my stomach as her voice dropped. "I've got plans for him."

My head was already drowning from her words and her touch, but when her hand moved lower, curling around my

. . .

"Cora!" I jolted, sounding like a pubescent boy. A moment later, after I'd sort of regained my senses, I glanced at her to find her giving me an odd look. Like she was confused.

"I'm sorry. I didn't mean to . . ." Her head turned away, and she leaned back into her seat.

Tell her, Matt. Tell her now. Perfect segue.

"No, it's fine." *It's really fine.* "You just surprised me. It's been a long day, and I'm not feeling like myself." I tried not to think too much on the irony of that sentence.

I found her hand and pulled it into my lap. More toward my knees than my package though, because damn, Cora's touch was not something to underestimate. If she so much as brushed her hand around my general zipper region again, I would be in a predicament. An I-just-got-off-from-a-woman-barely-touching-me kind of predicament.

"Then make sure to get some rest on the flight." When her eyes met mine, my stomach lurched. "It's going to be a long night too."

Saying nothing else, she dropped her head onto my shoulder, nudging at my arm until I got the hint. Folding my arm around her back, I drew her close, and I swore to god, if I could have just spent the rest of my life like that, I would have been a happy man.

She shifted against me, her expression hesitant. "Are you sure Matt's okay? I feel awful that he got so sick today."

I smiled into the dark limousine. She was thinking about me. She was with him but thinking about me. It made me wonder if that had ever happened before, and if so, how many times?

"Yeah, it was probably some bad sushi or something. You know how that guy is with his raw fish."

Cora nodded against my shoulder. "He was okay when you guys went to bed last night, right? When you stayed at his place?"

There was just enough doubt in her voice for me to pick up on. She was questioning if Jacob had really stayed the night at my place. If he'd gone to bed like a good boy on the night of his wedding, or spent it partying like he tended to most Friday nights.

Tell her now. Another segue that's as good as they're going to get.

"Yeah, it wasn't until this afternoon when he started losing his insides via his mouth." I sighed to myself after. Every minute that went by made it harder to tell her.

"We should swing by, you know? Bring him some tea or soup or something." She tipped her head so she was looking up at me.

My chest squeezed. She wasn't just thinking about me, she wanted to do something for me. She wanted to do something nice for me on her wedding day. It was no wonder I'd had it so bad for Cora all of these years. No woman rivaled her. No woman ever could.

"Believe me, it would come right back up. And if we want to make our flight, we can't waste another minute." I checked my watch. We had plenty of time before our flight to make a quick stop, but there wouldn't be a food-poisoned Matt to check on if we did stop.

"Then let's call him." Cora was already pulling her phone out of her purse.

"No!" I wrapped my hand around hers before she could dial my number. My phone was currently in my pants' pocket and not silenced. "Let him rest. We'll call him in the morning." *Yeah, brilliant. Delay the inevitable, because you haven't already dug yourself a good and deep hole.* "I've got his wedding present for us," I said to shift the conversation. "He gave it to me earlier."

When I pulled the silver bracelet from my pocket, Cora sat up, studying it carefully. "That was your mother's."

Her fingers touched the charms hanging from the bracelet, charms representing memories of all the places we'd traveled together before she died. From one of Mickey Mouse from the time she'd taken us to Disney World, to a spaceship from when we'd visited Cape Canaveral.

"Why would he give it to me instead of his wife one day?" she asked as I clasped it into place on her wrist.

That question was one of the few I could answer honestly. "Because he loves you." I studied the bracelet on her wrist; it was a perfect fit. Then I glanced at the ring on her finger. I might have been the one who'd slid it into place there, but I wasn't the one she wanted. I never had been. "You're like the sister he never had and the wife he never will have."

Her head shook against me. "He'll find someone. I know it." She exhaled, almost sounding sad. Was it pity? Or was it regret? I couldn't be sure. "I can't believe someone hasn't snatched him up yet."

I snorted, like I knew Jacob would have. "Matt?"

"Yes, Matt." She blinked at me, one eyebrow raised. "Don't pretend you don't adore him. He's a good man. You *both* are good men. I just want to see him happy like we are."

Another break in my heart. It was a miracle there was still anything left to break after all of these years.

My arm tightened around her, my chin tucking over her head. "He is happy. I know it."

He'd never been happier.

At least for the moment.

CHAPTER THREE

Cora

I loved him more than ever before.

It was a relief, because I hadn't been sure how either one of us would feel once we were married. With some couples, it seemed like marriage made them fall more in love every day, and with others, more out of love.

Sitting in that limo, I knew for sure we were in that "more every day" category. I also knew I'd made the right decision. After everything—the doubts, the fights, the lies, the promises—I'd made the right decision. It was confirmed every time I looked into my new husband's eyes. He didn't just love me today—he'd love me forever.

He hadn't just spoken his vows—he'd *meant* them. That had been obvious from the way his eyes never left mine as he said them, and from the tone of his voice, strong and unwavering. I'd felt it when he slid on my ring, and I'd felt it when he kissed me for the first time as a married couple.

Damn, just thinking about that kiss was making me shift in place, the memory of it warming my heart at the same time it made something else heat up. Jacob had never really kissed me like he had today, and in front of hundreds of people no less. He kissed me like we'd been lovers in hundreds of lifetimes before this one, like he wouldn't rest until he found me in a hundred more lifetimes in the future. He kissed me like I was everything he needed, and I was clinging to the hope that I was.

Jacob and I had never had an easy relationship; I'd always assumed that was what made it so real. We weren't like the couples who acted like they'd never so much as fired a heated word at each other or doubted if they were with the right person. We'd never been the perfect couple, but we'd been an authentic one.

He had issues, I had issues, and we fought about our issues. Regularly.

When he'd asked me a year ago to marry him, I hadn't been able to answer right away. It had taken me two solid weeks of consideration and contemplation to give him my answer. Lately, I'd been doubting that I'd given him the right one. After today, I knew with certainty I had.

All of those doubts and mistakes, I'd leave in the past. He'd messed up, but I wasn't exactly innocent either. That wasn't what mattered anymore. I wouldn't focus on what was behind us but what was in front of us.

"You're quiet." I glanced at Jacob as we waited for our tickets to be taken. He still made my stomach drop when I looked at him, even though I'd been looking at him for two decades. The Adams brothers had made plenty of stomachs drop. A side effect of having a nice body and an even nicer face.

He handed the woman at the gate our tickets before roping his arm around me. "Sorry. There's a lot going through my head right now." That same heavy, burdened look cast over his face. It had made its appearance a lot today.

"Having second thoughts?" I lifted his left hand, tapping his wedding ring with my finger as we started down the breezeway to the plane.

"Second thoughts about marrying you? No way." His head shook. "But second thoughts about you marrying me? Maybe."

My forehead creased. I wasn't used to this thoughtful, brooding side of Jacob. He was more a fan of hiding his feelings than laying them out for me to see. "What do you mean?"

His breath came out all at once, like his lungs were collapsing on themselves. "Why do you love me? After everything I've put you through, why me?"

I waited to see if he was being serious. This was an odd time to bring up this kind of thing—hours after the wedding.

My silence was met with more from him, so I finally answered. "Because you're not the only one with faults. I've got mine too." My eyes closed when I thought of my own—my biggest fault had been a part of me for so long, I wasn't sure it was something I could ever move beyond. But I'd have to try, because we were married now and that changed everything. "And you and I, we've been through a lot together and you've always been there for me when it counted. When I needed you."

"You know you deserve better, right?" Jacob took my hand as we boarded the plane, making our way toward our seats up front.

"I know I want you. That's all that matters to me."

My hand tightened around his as we wove down the aisle and I concentrated on keeping my breathing even. I'd never been a fan of flying. Secretly. I'd flown a handful of places, usually for work, and never made a big deal about it to whomever I was traveling with. I usually chased a couple of Benadryl with a stiff drink before I boarded, but I'd gotten totally distracted by my new husband and the way it had taken him half an hour to pick out just the right charm at the duty-free jewelry store to add to my new bracelet. He'd gone with an eternity symbol, which was all kinds of perfect given the promises we'd made to each other today.

Then we'd wasted another half hour in a little dessert shop, sampling one of everything they had on display. Which was, again, all kinds of perfect since Jacob didn't usually like to indulge my sweet tooth. Something about wanting to keep me healthy, but I guessed it had also had something to do with wanting to keep me semi-thin. So usually I just satisfied my sweet cravings when I was alone and could take my time with whatever lovely confection I was in the mood for. Tonight's out-of-character displays led me to wonder if he was trying to demonstrate that he loved me no matter what. Those vows he'd said in that strong voice of his rolled through my mind again.

When we made it to our seats, he slid aside to give me the window seat. When he saw my face, concern drew his brows together. "What's the matter?" He slid in beside me right away, scanning my face like he was trying to figure out what was wrong.

"Um . . ." I'd never mentioned to Jacob my fear of flying. We'd only taken a couple of flights together, and he'd barely seemed to notice when I passed out from my antihistamine-vodka daze.

"Cora, what is it?" He looked worried. Like he was about to dial 9-1-1 or something worried.

"It's just flying and me. We don't really get along." My body was breaking out in a clammy sweat and the cabin door hadn't even been sealed. I'd brought my smaller clutch onto the flight, which did not contain an emergency supply of Benadryl.

"If you don't like flying, then why are we headed to St. Thomas for our honeymoon?" He scanned up and down the aisle like he was looking for something to help me.

"Because you wanted to go to St. Thomas for our honeymoon?" I answered, since it had been his idea. Jacob loved the Caribbean.

His jaw ground together at the same time his eyes narrowed like he was pissed about something. "Let's get off," he said, already rising in his seat.

"No." I grabbed his hand and pulled him back down. "I'll be fine. It's our honeymoon. I wouldn't miss it if it meant taking a twenty-hour flight."

"Cora . . ." His gaze swept back toward the door, where the last passengers were staggering in.

"I'll be okay. I've got you with me."

When my fingers tied through his, he exhaled. "How long have you been scared of flying?"

Honest answer? Then I reminded myself we were married. Honesty was the only way to go. "Forever."

Jacob's eyes lifted to the ceiling, his jaw doing that clamping thing again. Then he spun around in his seat and raised his hand. One of the first-class attendants appeared beside our row a moment later.

"Can you get her a drink, please?" he asked. "A good one?"

The attendant gave me a sympathetic look. "Of course. I'll be right back."

While she rushed off to get my drink, Jacob stood and shuffled through some of the overhead bins until he pulled a pillow and blanket out of one. "Here. Make yourself comfortable."

When the cabin door sealed shut, I jolted.

"Or as comfortable as you can be."

Jacob didn't bother with the cup when the attendant showed back up with an array of small bottles. He just twisted the cap off the first bottle and held it out for me, practically lifting it to my lips. He thanked the attendant, who was kind enough to pull a couple more bottles from her apron and set them on his armrest.

"I'm having flashbacks to our first date." I smiled then let him lift the bottle to my lips. It tasted awful, but hopefully it would go to my head quickly so I could fall asleep and stay asleep until we were in St. Thomas.

"Why flashbacks?" His brow cocked as he tipped the bottle back against my lips.

And just like that, I finished a mini bottle of disgusting vodka. On the plus side, I could already feel it making my head fuzzy. "Because you pretty much shoved one of those things into my mouth then too. Except it was a bigger bottle." I flicked the empty bottle he was screwing the lid back onto. "And after, we had our first kiss."

His hand froze, along with the rest of his body. It took me gently nudging him and squeezing his hand to break his sudden freeze.

"What did you expect? A girl like you wasn't going to kiss a guy like me sober." He smiled, but it was a conjured up one.

"You kissed me. Nice try." I twisted in my seat so I was facing him, feeling my nerves start to dull. That was when the plane started to move, and fresh adrenaline burst into my system. Before he could stop me, I grabbed another mini bottle and unscrewed the lid.

"But you kissed me back."

"Not that I had a lot of choice in the matter." I raised my eyebrows at him, remembering that night, and took a drink.

Concern drew up his face. "Are you saying I forced myself on you?" He cleared his throat as his hands worked into fists.

Okay, I'd been drinking that night, but it was one of the few nights Jacob hadn't been. He should have remembered our first date and kiss better than I did.

"No, you didn't force yourself on me. If you had, I wouldn't have let you put this shiny expensive thing on my finger this afternoon." I lifted my left hand, waving my fingers in his face. "But you were *forceful*." I paused, reliving the scene. It had been my first kiss ever, and while it was everything I'd always hoped it would be, it was, in another way, a giant letdown in the fireworks department. I'd never told Jacob that, and I never would. Some truths were better taken to one's grave than left to wither in the open air. "A force to be reckoned with. That's always been you, Jacob."

He was quiet, staring straight ahead like he was in a different world. When the plane started to take off, the jets blasting so loudly I felt the noise rattling my insides, I clamped my eyes closed and tried to find my happy place.

No amount of intoxication could erase my dread of takeoff and landing. I'd learned that long ago. The beginning and the end was always the worst—the scariest part.

Jacob's arm wrapped around my quivering body, and he drew me close. His head tucked over mine, and he pulled the blanket tight around my body, making me feel like nothing could happen as long as he was here.

It was a foreign feeling when it came to Jacob—feeling safe. Usually I felt more exposed with him, like I never knew what to expect or how to react. At the same time it was a new feeling for me to have with him, it was not a new feeling overall. I'd felt this way before, but it hadn't been in Jacob's presence—it had been in his brother's.

Matt.

God, I couldn't think of him. Not right now. Not now that I'd married Jacob and made things final between us. It wasn't fair to Jacob. It wasn't fair to either of them. It wasn't fair to me either. I'd waited. And waited. And nothing.

I'd been wrong about Matt harboring feelings for me. I'd been wrong to harbor my own. I'd kept Jacob on the line, biding his time, for too long, and I'd finally accepted what I should have long ago.

Matt didn't love me. Not the way I wanted him to.

So I'd agreed when Jacob asked me again last summer to marry him. I'd finally agreed to get on with my life and stop living it in some perpetual state of waiting.

I'd chosen Jacob. And sitting here beside him, having him comfort me and hold me close, confirmed that I'd made the right choice.

No one could love me the way the man holding me right now could.

CHAPTER FOUR

Cora

Could this driver be any slower?! I leaned forward to check the odometer to see if we really were traveling two miles per hour like it felt. Surprisingly, the odometer still showed we were cruising along in the thirty to thirty-five mile an hour range.

"What's up?" Jacob leaned forward with me to see what I was checking for—for the ten thousandth time since sliding into the backseat of the cab at the airport.

"Nothing. Just feels like we're going slow." My eyes narrowed on the odometer. At least I thought we were going about thirty-five; it was hard to tell. I'd finished more mini bottles of alcohol than a girl my stature probably should have during that two-plus-hour flight, but I'd made it and survived without going full-on psycho.

I'd blown past buzzed two mini bottles ago. Which meant my vision was a little funky.

"In a hurry to get somewhere?" Jacob's voice was low, his words like velvet, as his fingers scrolled down my arm, brushing the side of my breast on their return trip.

The touch surprised me, making me shift in my seat. He'd barely touched me today, which was very un-Jacob-like. He'd barely let me touch him either, which was even more un-Jacob-like. It was almost like my new husband had grown some Puritan values or something.

But no. He'd just grazed my breast. In the backseat of a taxi. I cleared my throat when his fingers repeated the motion, this time practically cupping my entire breast in his palm.

No, definitely not a Puritan value—squeezing one's wife's boob in the backseat of a cab. Thank god.

I turned my head so I was looking at him. He was staring at me with something dark in his eyes—something almost predatory. The ache between my legs grew until I felt like my whole being was consumed with need.

"You're making me in more of a hurry."

He kissed the tip of my nose, his fingers still touching me in ways that were making me squirm. "Good."

The warmth of whiskey on his breath broke across my mouth. The glaze in his eyes told me that I wasn't the only one who'd drank a little more than they should have on the plane ride. But he'd only had a couple of bottles, which should not have affected Jacob at all. I'd seen him down ten times as much in the same amount of time and still have enough coordination to play a game of Ping-Pong with his non-dominant hand. It was strange that two baby bottles would be getting to him the way they were, but maybe it was due to all of the excitement of the day. He probably hadn't eaten much, so those two bottles had gone straight to his head.

"Are you hungry? We could stop and grab something on our way to the hotel." I scanned outside the window for any convenience store or late night drive-through that might still be open. Not that St. Thomas was a mecca for fast food and 7-11s.

Jacob's arm wound lower, his hand lifting my hip so it could slide beneath me. He gave my backside a hard squeeze, pressing my body impossibly close to his. "I'm hungry for you."

His warm breath heated the skin below my ear right before his lips touched it. My back went rigid when he lightly sucked at my neck. He didn't stop until I knew he'd put a mark on me. I could already feel it rising to the surface. The proof that I belonged to this man pulled things from me that I hadn't known were there in the first place.

The cab driver was paying attention to the road, thankfully, but when a soft whimper spilled out of my mouth, his eyes lifted to the rearview. He must have guessed what was going on because his eyes flickered back to the windshield a moment after.

The hotel was up ahead. We'd just passed through the gates, and I could make out the massive structure Jacob had showed me online when he'd pitched St. Thomas as a honeymoon idea. I'd been happy to go with St. Thomas when the alternatives he suggested were Cancun, Crete, and Amsterdam. St. Thomas was the quietest of those options, although the resort was like its own mini party that never ended, from the looks of it.

That was probably why Jacob had picked it. If it had been up to me, we'd be on some quiet island where you maybe came across the occasional sea turtle.

"Penthouse?" Jacob said, glancing at the tall tower as the cab approached.

"Nothing but the best for you, right?" I could see that the lobby was full of people in bright clothes, drinks in hand and all-nighter goals in sight.

"Yeah, but what's the best for you?" Jacob pulled out his phone and pulled up the hotel's website. I wasn't sure how to answer that, so I stayed quiet as he scrolled through a few pages, getting ready to open the door. "I'll be right back. Just hang tight a minute."

Before I could say anything, he'd closed the door and was loping up the gleaming stairs of the hotel's entrance. He'd booked the penthouse a whole five minutes after we set the wedding date, wanting to make sure we had the top floor and everyone knew we had the top floor. So why was he acting like the penthouse wasn't going to work anymore? It wasn't like there was anything higher or more prestigious.

While I waited, I spun the bracelet around on my wrist. Only a few minutes later, he was back, climbing into the backseat with a half-smile.

"What?" I asked, nudging him.

He ignored me, his smile spreading as he listed off a few directions to the driver. The car pulled away from the curb, and we headed away from the monstrous tower.

"What in the world is going on?" I asked, twisting in my seat so he had to look at me.

Now he was practically grinning, like he was in on the best secret ever. His shoulder lifted. "The resort has a few cabins too. Private cabins on the outskirts of the property."

His eyes met mine as he lifted a couple of keys. "And lucky for us, they still had one available."

I couldn't help it—I started bouncing like a little kid in my seat. "Private cabin?"

"Private *beachfront* cabin."

More bouncing, but then I stopped. "But you wanted the penthouse. You booked it a year ago. Why did you change your mind?"

Jacob's arm came around me again. "Because what's best for me is what's best for *you*."

My heart did that skip thing it hadn't done in a long time. I knew how badly he'd wanted that room, so that he'd changed things so I'd be more comfortable reminded me again why I'd made the right decision marrying him.

Jacob Adams loved me. He'd had a difficult time showing it at times, but I'd always known he did, and today, he was finally proving it. I'd stood by him in the hard times, so I was going to enjoy these good times.

"Have I mentioned I love you?" I asked, dropping my hand against his chest. I felt his head shake above mine.

"No. I don't think you have."

I let go of the breath I'd been holding. I didn't need to hold my breath that everything would be okay anymore. "I love you," I whispered. "I love you so much."

CHAPTER FIVE

Matt

Standing in at the wedding had turned into standing in at the honeymoon. I wasn't exactly sure how I'd gotten here. Why I'd let it get this far. Why I hadn't pulled her aside at the reception to tell her what was up.

I knew part of it was because I didn't want to hurt her, but I couldn't ignore how this whole day felt so right. I had a conscience—I knew I did. Somewhere. It had made itself known plenty of times before where Cora was involved, but today, it seemed to have disappeared. Taken a temporary hiatus.

I supposed I should have been more concerned than I was.

Maybe now that we were about to finally be alone, I should tell her. She *might* never forgive me, but she definitely never would if we went into that cottage and something else happened. I had to tell her before we got to that point.

"Is this for real?" Cora squealed when the driver stopped in front of a dark cottage at the edge of the resort. I couldn't see anything else around but the beach, a few lonely palm trees, and an endless starry sky that bled into the still ocean.

"Better?" I said before sliding out of the cab and taking her hand to help her out. She was still reeling from downing a handful of mini bottles of airline booze. I wasn't exactly sober either.

"This is perfect." She smiled at the cabin as the driver stacked our suitcases outside of the door. "This day was perfect. And you are perfect."

I grunted. "I am completely *un*perfect."

She glanced back at me as she continued toward the cabin. "I'm not used to you not taking a compliment and being so modest. That's more your brother's style."

I focused on paying the cab driver. She knew us both so well—it was a damn miracle she hadn't figured it out sooner. I had wedding day anxiety and swarms of people and small bottles of alcohol to thank for her not realizing it, but tomorrow would be different. Tomorrow would be only her and me and no one to distract us, nothing to pull us apart. She'd figure it out. Jacob and I might have looked the same, but that was where our similarities ended.

I lingered at the bottom of the stairs after the cab left. She was waiting for me, but I knew what she was waiting for. She hadn't been subtle about it, and this was her wedding night. There were times in my life when I'd thought myself a strong man—like the first time I saved a life in the ER or helped an injured passenger at the scene of an accident—but never when it came to Cora. Not once. I would abandon all of my supposed morals and beliefs to protect her. My beliefs about what was right and wrong became intermingled with my complete and total adoration of the woman standing before me, waiting.

Waiting for me to carry her inside and make love to her.

I'd have given her anything, but I couldn't give her this. Because it wasn't me she was asking. It was Jacob. Always Jacob.

"Well?" She held out her hand, a gleam in her eyes that made every muscle in my body ache. When I took a moment to meet her in front of the door, she absently twirled the charm bracelet. "Do you remember the time my mom took us all to Disney World and both of you were fighting over who got to ride with me on Magic Mountain? And I said I'd ride with you both so you'd stop fighting?"

"Yeah," I answered, climbing the stairs. "I remember you picking Matt first."

Her eyes lifted, like she was familiar with this type of jealousy. God knew she'd seen no shortage of it growing up with us. "But then you threw a fit, so I went with you first and Matt second."

I nodded as I stuck the key in the lock. "And he never stopped reminding me how you just wanted to save the best for last."

She laughed gently, then her face ironed out all at once. "Sorry. I shouldn't be talking about him right now. I know it makes you uncomfortable."

My brows pulled together after I opened the door. "Why does you talking about Matt make me uncomfortable?"

Cora shifted. "Because."

"Because why?"

She sucked in a breath. She was in the middle of letting it out when she said, "Because you've always been under some impression that I'm into him. You've never liked me talking about him, or even talking with him."

I'd been about to grab the suitcases, but I stopped. More like I froze. Jacob had been under some impression that Cora liked me? He'd never said anything to me—never even indicated anything that would make me think he didn't want her around me. "Please. When have I not wanted you to talk with my brother? We grew up together."

Cora's hand settled above her hip as she blinked at me. "Are you really going to make me recap the past decade for you? Because that might take the next decade to sum up."

For real? Jacob had never hinted at Cora having feelings for me, but clearly he'd brought it up to her. Plenty of times, from the sound of it. Which was its own kind of surprise. But Jacob believing she might have harbored feelings for me didn't mean she actually did. That was all I really cared about. Not my brother's tendency toward jealousy.

"So?" I crossed my arms and leaned into the banister behind me. "Did you? Like my brother?"

She sighed, turning toward the open door. "Jacob . . ."

"What? It's a fair question." I shoved off the banister, feeling hope and heat tangling in my veins from the look on her face, from the sound of her voice. She'd felt *something* for me, whether it be the most passing of crushes or something much deeper. Realizing that had me feeling drunk from something other than alcohol. "Besides, you're stuck with me now. Won't matter what you 'fess up to."

Cora started through the doorway. "I don't want to talk about it."

Grabbing the suitcases, I followed her. I wasn't letting this go. Never. Not if she threatened death or castration or anything else. "Why not?"

She broke to a sudden stop a few feet inside the room. "Because I don't want to focus on the past. I want to concentrate on the future. That's not going to work if you keep asking me questions about Matt."

There was a sharpness in her voice—one she didn't use too often. She didn't want to keep talking about me, which only made me want to continue talking about me. I'd struck a nerve, but I wasn't sure how deep that nerve went.

I *needed* to know how deep it went. I had to know. My whole life, I'd been under the impression that Cora saw me as nothing more than a good friend and substitute brother. She cared for me, but not in the same way I cared for her.

Or did she?

"This thing with Matt . . ."

Her back stiffened.

"Was it a thing? Like ancient history? Or is it still a thing?" I closed the door and wondered why I could feel my heartbeat in my eardrums.

She kept her back to me, standing in the middle of the dark room like a lone ship on a vast ocean. "I married you."

Yeah, she did marry me.

"But if he'd made a play for you, way back before all of this"—I waved my finger between the two of us, not that she could see it—"would you have given him a chance?"

"He never made a play for me." Her voice sounded faraway, like she was out of reach when she was less than an arm's length away.

"That doesn't answer my question." I stepped closer. "If he had? Would you have?"

Her back was moving faster from her quickened breathing. This conversation was making her uncomfortable. Why was that?

"Stop, Jacob. Enough." She spun on me, swaying in place just enough that I reached out to steady her. She shook my hand away like it was white-hot. "I'm not going to get into another fight with you over Matt. I'm done. I picked you. I married you. What else do I have to prove?"

"That you don't—"

"I don't love Matt!" Her arms flung out at her sides as her voice spilled across the room. 'There. I said it. Are you happy now? Are you happy we've managed to get into another argument over this infatuation you're convinced I have for your brother? On our wedding night of all times?" She glared at me with bleary eyes. I couldn't tell if that was from tears or from alcohol. Maybe both.

"Cora, I'm sorry." I ran my hands through my hair, wondering what in the hell I was doing—for the millionth time that day. Deceiving her, betraying her, and now accusing and angering her. Maybe I didn't know the first fucking thing about love. Maybe Jacob knew more about it than I did, because I wasn't sure love was supposed to hurt as badly as this did.

"Just . . . enough already." As she shouldered past me, I reached for her, but she shook me off. "I need to be alone."

She slammed the front door behind her a moment later, leaving me alone with my idiocy.

"Cora," I called to an empty room. I wasn't thinking when I rushed toward the door after her. "Cora!"

The moment I pulled the door open, something crashed into me. It made a sharp breath rush out of my mouth as I staggered back a few steps.

My arms barely had time to wrap around her before Cora's mouth was on mine, moving in such a way that made staying upright next to impossible. Before I had a chance to catch up to the fact that I was kissing Cora in an entirely different way than we'd kissed at the wedding and reception, her fingers were working at my belt. Quickly.

I didn't know she'd already gotten it undone before she'd moved on to my zipper. The sounds she was making as she kissed me, the way her body felt aligned against mine, the way her mouth knew the intricate balance of submission and domination . . . one moment at a time, Cora was crushing the last remnants of my resolve. Destroying the final pieces of my views of right and wrong.

My arm stretched out to brace against a porch beam, Cora clinging to me like I was trying to cling to my senses, and that was when I saw it. The thick shining band on my finger. That wedding band might have been on my finger, but it wasn't meant for me.

Cora might have been tangled around my body, but she wasn't meant for me either.

"Wait." I didn't recognize my voice. I didn't want to acknowledge my demand. "Cora—stop."

Her mouth slowed, but her lips hovered against mine. Her fingers slowed . . . but they didn't stop. A throaty groan echoed in my chest when her hand slipped through my zipper, cupping a part of my anatomy that felt like it had, at present, taken over my mental capacity.

"I don't want to argue with you," she breathed against my mouth. "I don't want to feel distant from you. Not tonight. I want to be close. I want to be part of you. I want you to be part of me." Her hand moved against me, slowly and methodically, and I felt like my lungs were about to explode. Kind of the way a balloon pops when too much air has been added. "I want a part of you inside me. Please." Her mouth lifted to my ear, my back trembling when her breath warmed my skin. "*Please.*"

I'd never been able to resist Cora whenever she'd asked me for something. Never once. Whether it was the time we were kids and she'd asked me to eat her Brussels sprouts so she didn't have to, or when we'd been older and she asked for a ride to the movie theater to meet some friends. Feeling like such a strong person in so many areas of my life was a hard thing to reconcile with how totally and utterly weak I felt in one area—her. Always her. She was as much my strength as she was my weakness. My best memory and my worst regret.

Cora had yet to request something of me that I'd failed to give her. I doubted if she ever would.

This time included.

My answer didn't come as a verbal one, but I wasn't sure responses came any clearer. Pressing into her, I backed her into the thick beam of the porch my arm was still braced against, still trying to keep me from falling out of whatever dream I'd landed in. When her body was as fitted against me as it was against the beam, I hoisted her up so I was looking her in the eyes. So I could press my hips between hers as her legs wound around my back.

A ragged exhale spilled from her mouth when I ground myself against her. I did it again, desperate to pull the same sound from her. Drunk with the feeling of knowing I could make her feel the way I did. Her chest rose and fell hard, writhing against me, lost in the same crutches of lust I was overtaken by.

My arm wasn't braced against the beam any longer. It wound around her, clinging to her body like it was my only salvation left in this world. My mouth covered hers when the next breath trembled from her. I reveled in the taste of her lips on mine, the feel of her tongue against mine.

Cora was everything I'd fantasized she would be, and nothing I ever thought I'd get to experience. I'd expected nothing, and here I was, getting everything.

Her hips tipped back from mine, just enough for her to free my dick, then her lap was burrowing into mine again. Except this time . . .

"Oh, god, Cora." My forehead fell into the beam in front of me. "Fuck," I breathed, feeling like my heart was about to break out of my chest from the way it was hammering.

"Easy access." I felt her smile curve against my lips as she took me inside her, millimeter by painstaking millimeter. "That's the way you like me, right, baby?" She trembled in my arms as she continued to take me.

All I could do was stand there, my fingers curling into her, my lungs about to collapse, and try to hold still while the woman of my dreams fucked me one unhurried inch at a time.

A weaker man couldn't have withstood it, and would have taken control and rammed the rest of the way inside the perfect body he was presently experiencing. A stronger man would have put a stop to this before we'd gotten here—here being me fucking my brother's girl on their wedding night.

"You're not the kind of woman who needs to make anything easy for any man. You're the kind who should make a man work for it. Make him work to earn your anything."

My chest was moving hard and quickly along with hers. My eyes squeezed shut when she stopped sliding down me, having no farther to go. She moaned when her legs tightened around my back, managing to draw even more of me inside her.

I wasn't going to last long. If long could even be ascribed to the embarrassing number of seconds it would take for Cora to get me off if she kept me deep inside her while she ran her hands down my body the way she was.

"What are you saying? You've changed your mind on your preference of me being easily accessible to you whenever and wherever?" Her lips grazed up my neck, pausing just below my jawbone to nip at a tender patch of flesh.

I flinched against her, which had me pulling out of her. This time it was me who controlled the rate of our fucking—and it wasn't slow and gentle this time. Both Cora's and my cries echoed into the night as I seated myself deep into her welcoming body.

"I'm saying you're worth every battle. Every challenge." I moved my face in front of hers so I could look her in the eyes. God, having her eyes on me when I was buried inside her was the single most erotic thing I'd ever felt. I could already feel my orgasm building, and I'd barely thrust twice into her. "You're worth ever bead of sweat and every groan of frustration. You're worth the work, you're worth the wait, you're worth everything I have to give you." I moved closer, so our foreheads were pressed together, our eyes aligned. "So make me work for it. Make me work hard for it. I will. You won't hear one complaint from me working myself to the bone for you. Not one." My hand slipped up her waist, molding around her breast, and my thumb played with her aroused nipple. "Make me work for it, Cora.

Don't make it easy, make it hard. Make it so fucking hard I feel like I just might die if I don't get to be with you."

Cora's head fell back as I continued to palm her breast, her hands bracing on my shoulders as she started to slide off me. "I think I already make it hard. So fucking hard."

She slid back down on me, and a breath hissed from my teeth as I felt close to blacking out. If she did that once more, I wouldn't be able to control myself. I'd be going off inside Cora for real this time, instead of imagining it like I did whenever I'd taken my dick into my hand. My release would be spent in her body instead of wasted in my sheets. Some part of me would be inside her after this. Forever.

That thought alone almost had me going off inside her right then.

"You could make my dick fucking hard on your worst day, baby. You've got no worries there." I circled my hips against her, reminding her of just how hard she made things for me. "But you make the rest hard too. Make me work for you. Make me earn your love. It's worth whatever price. Whatever cost. Don't let me come to expect easy with you. Make me want to work hard for you."

The way she was squirming in my arms from the way I was touching her breast, her back bowing whenever I pulled at her nipple, had me reaching for the neckline of her dress and yanking on it.

The sound it made when ripping didn't jolt either of us, and neither did the sounds of small buttons skipping across the wood porch. I felt my dick kick inside her when I took my first look at her naked breast on display. Perfect. That was the only way to describe Cora, from the person she was as a whole to her right breast glowing in the moonlight. Her nipple managed to harden even more from the cool night air whispering around it, or maybe it was from the way I was staring at it, my jaw grinding in an effort to keep from coming right then.

"Put me in your mouth." Cora's chest was still rising and falling hard, but her voice was even, her eyes unblinking as she made her request. She must have seen something on my face she read as surprise, because her eyebrow rose. "You told me to make things harder on you. Then I guess that means I need to be more vocal about what I want and less willing to just give you what you want."

It looked like she might have been about to add more, but all manner of speech was rendered incapacitated when my mouth fell to her breast, sucking her nipple. It must have surprised her, because the loudest cry I had yet to draw from her fell from her mouth, so loud I wondered how far it would travel across the ocean. One of her hands came around my head, her fingers tangling in my hair as I worked her over in my mouth. I became a student in that minute, studying her for signs of pleasure, watching for signs of ecstasy, committing to memory the way her body bucked against mine when my teeth sank into the delicate, prickled flesh.

The sounds she made for me as I made love to her body, I'd never forget. The way she submitted to me, letting me do whatever I wanted at the same time I realized just how much she was demanding of me in that moment of unabashed intimacy, she had me questioning if what I'd done, and what I was doing, was really so reprehensible.

Who I was or wasn't didn't change the way this woman was responding to me right now, in this moment. It didn't changed the way she writhed in my arms, begging me to give her what she wanted as I felt her desire run down her legs. For this moment in time, this infinite journey between one moment to the next, we were meant to be together. The time between two seconds was immeasurable, and though I knew our moment would come to an end, it would be a limitless one. We were two halves of one being who had at last found each other and come together in this union.

"Please. *Please*," she breathed, begging me with her eyes as well when I looked up to meet them. "Come with me. I want our first time as husband and wife to be together."

When I released her nipple, I felt my inner demon gloat when I saw it was red and wet, compliments of my mouth. "Are you asking me to fuck you? Do you want me to stop fucking around and just fuck you now?"

Her throat bobbed, her eyes going wide like she wasn't expecting these words from me. At the same time, she looked like she liked them. "Yes. That's what I want." Her legs tangled around me again, her lap circling mine in a way that made my eyes roll back into my head.

"Are you close, baby?" I grunted, clenching my fists in an attempt to keep from going off. "Because I am. I'm so close, you do that again, and you're going to be in trouble."

"You're that close?" Her mouth was back on my neck, kissing it between her words, but I didn't miss the note of disbelief in her voice. I didn't get it though. As it was, it was the miracle of this lifetime I hadn't already lost it inside her yet.

I tipped my head back to give her better access to my neck. God, I hoped she'd put a couple of marks on me like I already had on her. I wanted Cora's mark on me for everyone to see. A mark of the physical variety, because her mark had been all over me in every other way.

"Closer," I breathed when I felt her tighten around my dick after my fingers dug deeper into her backside. Moving my other hand between us, I slid it under her dress, only one destination in mind.

The moment my thumb circled the sensitive spot, I felt her orgasm unfold. Her body went rigid on mine at first, her body pulsing around me, as her moans turned to cries.

"Tell me you want it, Cora." I ground my jaw as her orgasm spilled through her body, taking everything inside me to keep from following her. "Tell me you want me."

Her hands dug into my shoulders as she rode me, pulling me deep inside her with every thrust, making me feel like the damn ruler of the universe from the way she was getting off. I'd never known pleasure existed the way I could see it playing out on her face. The way I could feel it pulsing around my damn dick.

"I want it." She panted, her chest bouncing as she pumped against me. "I want *you*."

That was all I needed to hear. She could have stopped bouncing on my dick and gone rigid, and I still would have come. Those were the words I'd dreamed of hearing come from Cora since she'd first come into my life. I'd wanted her to want me the way I wanted her. I knew she might have been referring to it in a different way, given our present situation, but it didn't change the words she'd spoken or the way I'd taken them.

I want you.

My orgasm hit me hard and violently, like it had been building for years and it had just burst free of whatever wall had been damming it up. Pinning her hard against the porch beam, I drove into her so hard she slid up the smooth wood beam a foot with every thrust. The whole time my release went off in her body, I forced my eyes to stay open so I could watch her. So I could remember the way she looked as I took my pleasure from her, and she took hers from me.

So if the rest of my life was as pathetically lonely as it had been up to now, I'd have this memory to get me through the long years. It would be enough. This moment would be enough for any man.

Even after my orgasm was long over, I kept my body moving inside hers, reveling in the new sensations. The way every muscle in her body felt spent and soft, supple and submissive. The way the union of our pleasure felt between my legs.

It took me forever to catch my breath. It took her just as long. The whole time, I held her, keeping her close as her body floated down from the high we'd just climbed.

She was still breathing deep, heavy breaths when she smiled. "Wow."

I knew what I'd just done. I knew what it meant. I should have been feeling guilty and ashamed and everything in between. I should have felt like whatever hopes I'd ever had of deserving this woman, whose body I was still sharing, was forever gone. But the thing about Cora was that no mortal man could ever hope to deserve her. They could only die trying. I was good spending whatever was left of my life doing just that.

"Yeah. Wow." I pulled her closer because I knew soon, I'd have to let her go. It made me want to hold her that much tighter now. "Let me just take this opportunity to apologize for the way we did it our first time as a married couple. I think I was supposed to make love to you instead of fucking you up against this thing, with most of our clothes still on, outside in the open. You make love to your wife on your first night together; you don't fuck her like some kind of animal."

She gave a contented sigh, before kissing the corner of my mouth. "I don't know what you classify that as, but that was the best sex we've ever had. No apology needed."

CHAPTER SIX

Cora

He was a different man.

I mean, he was still Jacob, but a different Jacob. There was a new meaning behind his words, the way his eyes matched what he was saying, the way he gave me his full attention instead of whatever fraction he had left over. I'd married a different man than the one I'd spent the past decade with, and I'd be lying to say if I didn't prefer this version. This was the Jacob I'd always hoped he'd become, even after I'd resigned myself to the fact that it was foolish to hold my breath waiting for a man to change.

His breathing was finally back to normal, but that could have been because he was fast asleep. After the porch . . . and the shower right after . . . and on the kitchen counter a little after that when we'd been attempting to refuel—he'd passed out into some kind of satisfied stupor. I should have too, but something was keeping me awake. *Him.*

I felt like I was afraid of falling asleep and waking up from this dream. The man I'd married wasn't the same one I'd spent half of my life with and I wanted more of these types of days—I wanted every day forward to be like this one—but I was superstitious too. So I didn't want to fall asleep, because if this was a dream, I didn't want to wake up to reality.

A couple of hours ago, he'd carried me to the master bed we were presently curled up in. After wrapping his arm around me and drawing me close, he'd kissed my forehead and fallen asleep. Even hours later, his arm was still folded around me, keeping my body beside his. Jacob had never been one for snuggling after sex. On occasion, he'd been known to indulge me, but it had never lasted for longer than a few minutes and never after he'd fallen asleep. He'd get too hot or develop a cramp in his arm or my hair would get in his mouth or some annoyance would set him off and he'd roll over and keep to his half of the bed for the rest of the night.

Something had changed, and I wasn't sure I knew what. I wasn't sure I needed to know what, because whatever it was, I approved. I didn't need to know the why to appreciate the result.

When I felt my eyes start to succumb to the heaviness they'd been battling, a yawn following right after, I leaned up on my elbow and tried blinking myself awake. It wasn't working. I'd been up for close to twenty-four hours, gotten married, survived a flight, and had repeated sex of the record-setting variety. It was going to take a miracle to keep me awake.

Or . . .

When my hand dropped to Jacob's stomach, my nails scrolling soft circles across the hard planes, I didn't miss the way he stirred in his sleep. The way a certain prominent, rather wonderful part of his body *stirred.*

Suddenly, I felt very much awake.

Not hesitating, I swung my leg over Jacob's lap, lining up our bodies until I felt his hardness pressing into me. As I lowered down over him, I bit my lip. I was a bit sore from all of our earlier exploits. It had been a while since Jacob and I had had sex back-to-back (to-back), and I was probably imagining it, but it seriously seemed like his dick had magically gotten bigger. At least it certainly felt like that, because, yeah, I hadn't been this sore since I'd lost my virginity to him back in high school.

When I was fully seated on his lap, I stayed still for a moment, giving myself a chance to adjust to his size. From his pillow, a lazy smile was moving into place as his even breaths indicated he was still asleep.

My hands molded into his chest as I moved over him. His skin was warm and smooth to the touch, but I loved how solid he felt below that warm, smooth surface. How firm and resilient and unmoving he seemed.

It wouldn't take me long—I'd discovered that earlier when Jacob had made that his mission—but this wasn't about me. This was about him. Taking care of him and putting him first, what marriage was all about. God knew he'd been proving that to me ever since we'd exchanged our vows.

The smallest of moans slipped out of me, but it might as well have been a scream from the way he jolted awake. Leaning up in bed, blinking awake, it took him a few seconds to catch up to what was happening. Once he took me in, naked and moving above him, his head fell back as every muscle in his body seemed to go rigid.

A sound rumbled deep in his chest—the kind of primal echo that made me have to slow my pace so I didn't come right then.

"I was having this exact dream," he gritted out, one hand finding the perch of my hip and holding on.

Hearing that made me smile. "How does the real version compare to the dream one?" To sway his answer, I circled my hips a couple of times, drawing another one of those primal sounds from him.

"The dream was a fucking joke compared to this." His head fell back into his pillow when my nails dug into his chest. "That's how they compare."

My smile spread. "Good to know. Plus, with dreams, right when you're about to get to the really good part, you wake up." I could tell he was close. From the way the muscles in his neck were pushing against his skin, to the way his pupils were wide, his eyes excited—he wouldn't last much longer.

"The best part of anything is being with you." His jaw set as my own orgasm tore through my body. "The best part is you."

It was his words. It was his body. It was the way his eyes held mine and matched the words coming from his mouth. I was trying to hold back, to wait until I'd given him his, but it was futile when he touched me the way he was, looking at me like I was every answer to every question.

The moment I cried out, his release thundered to the surface. His hands braced against me like mine were against him, holding on to each other as though we were the only thing keeping each other tethered to this world.

When we finished, he gathered my body against him, both of our chests coated with sweat, our lungs laboring. He held me like that until I could just make out the first ribbons of light breaking through the dark sky. It was a new day. A new life.

As his fingers combed through my tangled mess of hair, his head turned toward mine to watch the sky lighten and the new day unfold. "Cora?" My body lowered as he let out a long exhale. His fingers stopped moving through my hair. "I need to tell you something."

My throat bobbed, knowing from his tone that this was something significant. I had a few ideas what my new husband might want to confess to me, but not yet. I didn't want to break the spell we'd managed to cast temporarily. I wanted honesty and openness from my husband. Maybe just not right after the single best night we'd ever shared together. Especially not the kind of honest I guessed Jacob had in mind to tell me.

"Not right now," I whispered, closing my eyes. The new day could wait. "Let's not ruin it. Not yet."

Another exhale, this one longer than before. His arms formed like vises around my spent body, but this hold was different. This was the hold of a man who was desperately clinging to something he knew would be ripped from his arms no matter how hard he held on.

"Whatever you want." His lips skimmed along my temple as he inhaled. "Whatever you need."

CHAPTER SEVEN

Matt

Holy fuck.

That was the first thing that burst into my head as I woke up later that morning. I'd just slept with my brother's girl. Repeatedly.

It wasn't just Jacob I'd betrayed though. It was Cora too. My betrayal toward her was the worst because she trusted me and yesterday . . . last night . . . she'd shared things with me, she'd shared her body with me, thinking I was Jacob. All of these years, I'd despised my brother for not realizing what a great thing he had in her, and here I'd just pretended to be him and slept with her.

It was official. I was going to hell. Every kind that had been invented and every one that existed. But who was I kidding? I'd been in hell for years. If this was what hell felt like, I was never packing my bags and leaving.

But I knew that when I told her, she'd hate me. She'd never look at me or speak to me again. Accepting that made me content to delay the inevitable, if only for five more minutes. Especially with the way she was holding onto my arm, cradling it to her chest like a child would cling to a stuffed bear for comfort.

As I lay there pretending like this moment wasn't coming to an imminent, disastrous end, I wondered what was going on back home. Had Jacob resurfaced? If so, had he put the pieces together yet? If he had, he'd be on the next plane he could catch to get here to kick my ass. Before that happened, I needed to tell her. I guessed it would go over marginally better than the man she thought she'd married showing up with murder in his eyes and a bare ring finger.

I needed to check my phone, to see how many missed calls and texts I'd gotten so I knew what was coming and how much longer I had. Trying to shimmy and slide out from Cora's embrace without waking her took about fifty different maneuvers, but it worked. She never even stirred as I crawled out of the bed where I'd realized the majority of every fantasy I'd dared to dream. That was where they'd have to stay though.

My phone was still tucked into the back pocket of my pants, which had been torn off somewhere in the middle of the room and had gotten kicked into . . .

The bathroom, I discovered after a minute of searching the cabin. Convenient, I thought as I closed the door so I could have some privacy to see just what kind of shit storm was brewing.

A glance at my phone revealed not one missed call or text. Not a single one. Not even from the hospital, which was rare since I was used to fielding at least a few daily calls from my coworkers and administrator. I exhaled, rubbing at my day's worth of stubble. The silence must mean no one knew yet. Jacob was still "indisposed." God only knew how much longer he'd remain in that state.

I wished it could be for the rest of forever. Because maybe if Jacob never surfaced from his stupor to realize he'd missed his own damn wedding, and if Cora never figured out I was the other brother, we could all just live happily ever after.

For a whole day and a half.

I drove my palm into the bathroom wall as I accepted there was no good way any of this could turn out. No matter what happened or how Cora found out, it was going to be catastrophic.

From chart-topping high to record-setting low.

Best day ever? Nice knowing you. Time to move over and get acquainted with worst day ever.

I was so consumed with my thoughts that I didn't register the sound of knocking at first. It was far off, too inconsequential for me to give much headspace to it in my present state of the-world-is-over.

"Breakfast. Thank goodness. I'm starving." Cora's sleepy voice cut through some of my haze, but it wasn't until I heard her padding around the room that I registered what was happening. "Why don't I let our breakfast in, then I'll join you in the shower in a sec. Do you have money for a tip in your wallet?"

The moment she said it, I started moving. Fast. It wasn't fast enough, I discovered, after throwing the bathroom door open to find Cora standing beside the nightstand, a white sheet twisted around her body, staring at my open wallet in confusion.

Shit. So not how I'd planned this going. Not that any of my plans had been all that impressive.

"Why do you have Matt's driver's license?" Cora blinked at the ID like she was trying to make sure what she was seeing was real.

I didn't know what to say. She still thought I was Jacob.

She slid a couple of cards out of their slots, each one drawing another crease into her forehead. "And why do you have Matt's credit cards too?"

In the background, I could make out the sound of knocking from whatever poor person was trying to deliver our breakfast with no idea what kind of storm was developing behind that closed door.

"Jacob?"

It wasn't until she looked at me again that she realized it. It wasn't until she saw whatever look was on my face that she figured out what Matt's wallet was doing in her hands the first morning of her honeymoon.

"Oh my god." The wallet dropped to the floor as she backed away from me. "Please, no. Please god no." She was whispering, almost like she was talking to herself, tears starting to streak down her cheeks as she continued separating herself from where I stood frozen in the bathroom doorway.

"Cora, please . . ." I swallowed, realizing I'd just had everything I'd ever wanted and was losing it all, all at once.

"Matt?" It sounded like less of a question and more of an accusation. "Oh my god. It is you, isn't it?"

She didn't wait for me to confirm it—I supposed she saw swimming in my eyes all she needed to be convinced of my guilt. I managed to move a whole step before I watched her hand reach for the front door.

"Cora, let me explain." I couldn't let her go. Not before I explained why I'd done it. Not before I apologized for what I'd done. Not before I handed her a knife to stab my heart or cut off my damn dick. Whatever it took to prove just how sorry I was that I was so impossibly hopeless when it came to her.

"Let you explain?" she repeated with disgust, looking at me like she didn't recognize me. Or more like she couldn't stand the sight of me. "Let you explain why it's you I'm waking up to the morning after my wedding? Instead of Jacob?" She let that settle between us, successfully making me feel like the piece of shit I knew I was. "Whatever your explanation is, I don't want to hear it. I just want to get out of here. Away from you. Off of this goddamned island."

She had the door thrown open and herself through it before the look of surprise could form on the server's face. He was still waiting outside the door, a covered tray in hand.

"Cora, wait!" I shouted, chasing after her.

She didn't wait though. She didn't even look once over her shoulder to see if I was following her. She rushed down the stairs and sprinted down the beach, the sheet billowing around her as she ran. She disappeared from sight while I stood at the top of the porch, watching her go. The story of my goddamned life.

I'd forgotten all about the server who'd brought us the breakfast order I'd put in last night until he cleared his throat. "Would you like me to leave this on the table, sir?"

When I looked back over my shoulder to find him clearly trying to avoid looking in my general area, I remembered my present state. My naked present state. "Yeah, that works."

I turned to go back into the cabin. I didn't take the time to cover myself with my hand or the throw pillow resting on the chair right inside the door. I just hustled to gather up my clothes spread around the room, tugging them on as I came to them. I needed to find her. I needed to get to her before she left this island. I needed a chance to explain, because I knew if she left before I did, I'd never get that chance. She'd avoid me at all costs from now on. She wouldn't attend any gatherings I might be at; she'd cross the road if she saw me walking down the same sidewalk as her. Hiding in Miami would be much easier than here on this island, especially while she was wearing nothing but a hotel sheet.

I needed to find her.

"Sir?"

Even though I was mostly dressed now, the server was still not about to make eye contact. Not that I could blame him after the scene he'd just witnessed.

"Yeah?" I stuffed my damn wallet into my pocket as I shoved my feet into my shoes.

"A storm warning has been issued for the island. Nothing to be too alarmed over, but the hotel's letting all of the guests know."

My brow furrowed, for the first time registering what time of the year it was and where Brother Dearest had elected to bring his new bride on their honeymoon. Because who didn't think Caribbean when they thought of October?

Probably explained why they'd had an extra cabin available so last minute.

"A storm as in a hurricane?" I asked, my gaze shifting out the open door. The skies were blue, and other than the gentle breeze playing with the palm leaves, that was all the wind to be found.

"It hasn't been classified a hurricane yet. It has only just started to form and it could change directions. Or die out completely before it hits land, so please don't let it worry you too much. The hotel wanted our guests to be aware, but we'll keep everyone up to date." The server managed a contrived smile as he backed out of the room after arranging two breakfasts at two empty chairs. "Just relax and enjoy your honeymoon, Mr. Adams."

I almost laughed at that. Relaxing was not in the plans for me any time soon. "Thanks for letting me know. Now if you'll excuse me . . ." I put aside all worries about some possible hurricane forming out on the ocean this island was smack in the middle of. That storm paled in comparison to the one I was already immersed in.

"Everything okay?" The server asked as he followed me through the door, glancing at the spot where Cora had disappeared into the palms.

"Not exactly. She just found out she married the wrong guy." *Literally.* I slid out a twenty to give him. "If you see a pretty girl in a white sheet . . ."

"I know who might be interested in her whereabouts." The server took the tip then jogged down the stairs and headed in one direction while I went the other.

Cora was fast, but she was barefoot and wearing a bulky sheet. She couldn't have gotten far, I told myself, even though I knew better. I wouldn't put it past her to go slide into a packed mass of people if she thought it would keep me from finding her. She could be anywhere, and she had a few minute lead on me.

Part of me wanted to rush to the airport to cut her off, because I knew that would be her eventual destination. She'd want out of here via the first flight she could find. But

I didn't want to have this conversation in an airport, where security would probably intervene before she got her second punch thrown. Cora had one hell of a right hook. I'd never been on the receiving end, but I'd watched Patrick Henry get knocked unconscious the Monday after Winter Formal, freshmen year. I'd been looking for him after I heard the rumors he'd spread about just how much Cora had put out that night. Cora beat me to him though, and I guessed she had more right than I did to take Patrick Henry down after what he'd said. But that hadn't stopped me from sweeping his feet out beneath him the next day as we passed in the hallway, half of his face swollen from Cora's fist.

I wanted her to hit me. I hoped she would. I might not have been Patrick Henry, but fuck, what I'd done put me way beneath him.

I tried to change my thoughts. They weren't helping, and I had the rest of my life to make myself feel like shit. I needed a clear head right now to find her and explain why I'd done it. I needed all my mental faculties firing on all engines when and if I found her. I wasn't expecting her to understand why I'd done it, but I needed her to *know* exactly why I had. It wasn't forgiveness I was looking for; it was something else.

But for right now, I just needed to find her.

CHAPTER EIGHT

Cora

Matt. I'd married Matt. Oh my god, I was his wife and we'd spent all night consummating that union.

My forehead banged against my bent knees as the reminder tore through my mind. What in the hell had happened? How had I not known? Where was Jacob? What did this mean? Was our marriage binding even though I thought I'd been marrying someone else? Would Jacob ever forgive me once he found out?

A sob constricted my throat as I realized that because of this, I'd lose both of them. I'd lose the two people I loved most in the world in the same day because of what had happened. I already knew Jacob wouldn't forgive me. He'd accuse me of secretly knowing and bring up his long-standing suspicions of me always having some draw toward his twin. He wouldn't forgive me, and I couldn't expect him to, because I *should* have known. The man I'd spent the past twenty-four hours with was not the same one I'd spent the past decade with. He'd been a different man. Because he'd actually been a different one.

God, it was so damn obvious. The way he'd looked at me, the out-of-character gestures, the streak of sensitivity, the way he'd fucked me . . .

I banged my forehead harder against my knees when images from last night replayed in my head. How messed up was it that the best sex I'd ever had with who I thought was Jacob had been instead with Matt? How dumb was I to have not figured it out when instead of focusing on his own pleasure, mine had been the priority last night? I couldn't think of one instance when Jacob had waited for me to come before he had his. He usually collapsed over me and was half-asleep by the time I gave up on the idea or slid my hand between our bodies to take care of myself.

Jacob would never forgive me.

And I would never forgive Matt.

I'd lost them both. Just like I'd always feared. Just like I'd always somehow known I would, because what right did some girl from a single mom who worked as hired help have to think she had some claim to two men like Matt and Jacob Adams?

The dream had been a fantasy all along, just like I'd always known, and I'd finally been woken up.

I wasn't sure how much longer I could linger here, planted on this isolated perch overlooking the big ocean, still wound in the sheet I'd spent all night moving under with Matt's body.

Matt.

My eyes swam with tears all over again. I tried to strangle the feelings that came with those thoughts of him. I'd made my choice years ago. I'd waited for him, but I couldn't wait forever, especially not when I knew how Jacob felt about me and that his attention would only last so long. I'd rather have one, even if it wasn't the one I wanted most, than neither. I'd picked Jacob, and these feelings I'd harbored this whole time for Matt weren't fair to any of us.

If there was some way to rid myself of them, I would have, but I'd tried everything and come up short. It didn't matter how many times I reminded myself it wasn't Matt I wanted, I still found myself imagining him when Jacob's body crawled over mine in bed. It didn't matter how many ways I tried to avoid Matt, he was always there, reminders of him in every facet of my life. It didn't matter how many times I reminded myself he didn't want me, I still dreamed visions of him whispering those very words into my ear as his hands roamed the bends and planes of my body.

To hell with never being able to forgive Matt—I'd never be able to forgive *myself*.

Okay, okay, enough. No more emotions and tears. Think.

I needed to get out of there. Immediately. The one (or two) problems with that was I was currently dressed in a sheet and my purse with those handy things known as identification and credit cards were back in the cabin. Where the wrong twin I'd married was.

So basically, I was screwed. I'd just have to spend the rest of my life here, because there was no way I was going back into that cabin and confronting him. Mainly because I was too worried about what would happen when Matt and I were alone again. Now that I knew what we were capable of, what he was capable of . . . I didn't trust myself. It was like telling someone who'd been sober off heroin for two weeks to step inside a house full of heroin free for the taking. I knew my limits, and Matt was a hard, *hard* one.

I couldn't be alone with him again, because now, I couldn't claim ignorance. I knew who he was, and if I fell into bed with him again, I wouldn't be able to claim lack of knowledge as the culprit.

So I just sat there, arms wound around my legs, forehead tapping my knees, feeling completely and utterly lost.

That was when I heard someone crunching through the tall grass behind me. Instead of jolting with surprise, I clamped my eyes closed tightly and hunkered down a little more. I knew who it was. I knew of only one person who seemed to have a sixth sense for finding me.

"Cora."

The way he said it, almost sighing my name, made it seem like he was relieved he'd found me. Like he'd doubted he ever would.

"Go away, Matt," I gritted into the folds of the sheet. "Go away and *stay* away."

He was quiet for a moment, only the sounds of his footsteps moving closer. "I'm not going anywhere." His voice was firm, final sounding, like no matter what I said or did, he was going to say what he wanted to. "Not until you hear why I did it. Not until you know how I feel."

I didn't want to know how he felt. I didn't want to know why he'd done it. That was what I kept telling myself, although I couldn't convince myself of it. "Last night . . . I'd been drinking. You'd been drinking. We were both—"

"Let's make one thing clear right now," Matt interrupted. "You were not some drunken fuck last night. Not even close, so don't try to play it off like I was just another guy swimming in alcohol and looking to score." He paused like he was hoping that would get good and deep inside my brain. "I can't speak for you and how you were last night, but I was fully in control of my body and mind when I took you. Each and every time."

My heart picked up from hearing his words, thinking of what he was referring to. "Yeah, well, I was good and drunk. I don't remember a thing from last night." The lie sounded convincing enough to my ears—hopefully it would to Matt's as well. "All I remember is waking up today and finding your wallet when I was expecting to find Jacob's. The rest is a black hole of nothing."

He was quiet after that. So quiet I glanced back to see if he was still there.

"You don't remember anything?"

I huffed as if that was the most obvious thing. "Nothing."

Another stretch of silence. "You don't remember anything? Really? Not even the last time when you woke me up by—"

"No!" I interrupted, *definitely* not remembering that last time. Or at least definitely not wanting him to think I remembered it. "But I think it's safe to say I can figure out what happened, thanks to us both being naked when I woke up." I squeezed my eyes shut again when I remembered the last thing he'd said to me before I'd fallen asleep tucked against his body. "I don't remember, and if you'll just keep your mouth shut, I won't have to know just how . . . or how much . . . or any of the details associated with last night's mistake. I've got enough to deal with right now without having all of the gory details filled in for me."

Behind me, I heard him repeat the word I'd just fired at him. *Mistake*.

A mistake. That was what this was. It had to be.

"Why did you do it?" My fingers ran through my hair as I tried to take as logical an approach to this as one could. "What in the hell happened yesterday?"

Even before I finished asking, part of me already had the answer. Part of me already knew exactly what had happened yesterday to make Matt wind up standing across from me on my wedding day. Exactly what had been happening for years, what people had tried to tell me but what I hadn't wanted to believe. Jacob had always been a flirt, but I'd never wanted to believe it went beyond the lingering stares or suggestive smiles.

"Yesterday, before the wedding, I couldn't find Jacob." It was clear he was choosing his words carefully. I wasn't focusing on what he was saying so much as what he wasn't saying. "I figured something must have come up and I figured he'd show up soon, so instead of calling off the whole wedding because he'd been held up in traffic and forgotten to charge his phone, or whatever the hell happened, I just figured I'd step in temporarily."

My head was throbbing. There was an ache between my legs too, but God, I didn't want to focus on that or what I'd been doing, repeatedly, to cause it. "You'd just step in when I was supposed to be promising forever to the man I was marrying?"

"Looking back, I know I made the wrong choice," he said, exhaling. "But in the moment, when that church was packed full of people and they were expecting to find a groom waiting for you at that altar in five minutes, that was the best idea I was capable of coming up with."

His voice sounded clearer, which meant he was standing closer. I could feel his closeness. In a way, I'd always been able to tell when Matt was near, but I supposed after last night, I was aware of his nearness for another reason.

"But you didn't just 'stand in' for Jacob at the ceremony." The light breeze shifted into something stronger, pulling at the folds of my sheet.

I heard Matt move closer. "I know. That's how I planned it, but when Jacob didn't show up and I couldn't get ahold of him, I didn't know what to do. I wasn't sure when to tell you, or even what to tell you, so I waited. I figured by the time the reception was done, Jacob would have shown up. But when he didn't, when I found out . . . I didn't want to see you hurt. I knew Jacob wouldn't want to see you hurt. I just wanted to protect you from any more heartache."

"And your idea of protecting me from pain was having me marry the wrong guy then go on my honeymoon with me and fuck me?" I had to pause long enough to take a breath. "That's your definition of protecting me?"

His sigh didn't seem to end. "My best intentions went a little—*a lot*—off course. I didn't stroll up to that altar yesterday thinking or hoping last night would unfold the way it did."

Every time either one of us mentioned anything about last night, my mind went there. As a result, my body reacted to the memories. Like right now, I could feel my nipples hardening as I remembered the way he'd moved inside me, the way he'd demanded I look into his eyes each time he made me come.

I hated my body for reacting to him how it was. I hated him for being responsible for it.

"Sorry if I have a hard time buying that. I'm not exactly in a giving-the-benefit-of-the-doubt type of mood." Right then, the sun caught my wedding ring and blinded me. I wasn't sure what that meant, but it seemed pretty damn symbolic of something given my present situation.

"You have every right to hate me—"

"Damn right I do," I snapped, twisting the ring around so the diamond couldn't catch the light anymore.

"I had no right to do what I did. Any of it," he added, sounding ashamed for the first time.

"Why, Matt? Why did you do it?" I tipped my head back so I could make out his outline. "Why did you *really* do it?" I needed to know. I needed to know if he'd done it because he'd been trying to help me, or if it was because he couldn't help himself.

"I already told you why."

"Yeah, and now I'm asking you to cut the shit and give me the real reason."

He was quiet for so long, I almost thought he was going to tell me. "I don't see how me answering that will help either of us right now."

My heart stopped. I swore it stopped. What did he mean by that? What I hoped he did? Or something else?

When I realized what I was hoping for, guilt washed over me so fast and heavy I felt like I was drowning in it. Jacob. He was the one I'd been in a relationship with for years. He was the one I'd said yes to marrying. He was the one whose name was on the marriage certificate we'd filed at the courthouse. He was the one who loved me and wanted me to be his wife.

I couldn't fight off the voice chiming in my head that kept asking me why he was gone and Matt was here if that was the truth.

My breath came out all at once, like I'd been holding it forever. "Where's Jacob?"

He was quiet. His silence told me everything I needed to know. And nothing I wanted to acknowledge.

"Matt?" Finally, I made eye contact with him.

He was looking at me like he'd been expecting the question. "I don't know."

A breath seeped past my lips. Matt had been covering for Jacob for their whole lives, as quick to protect his brother as he was me. His experience had made him a proficient liar, but I knew that. I knew he was lying. Or withholding the truth.

What I didn't know was how bad that truth he was keeping from me was.

"Where is he?"

"I—"

"Yes, you do. You know where he is." My gaze dropped, unable to hold his stare any longer. "Or who he's with."

My voice had been so quiet, I didn't think he'd heard me. As silent as those words had been, I wished I could take them back. I wished I could swallow them back down into the dark hole they'd crawled from, because thinking it was one thing, but acknowledging it made it real.

Matt crouched behind me, keeping a careful distance when I tensed at his proximity to me. "If he's with anyone else when he's got you waiting for him, he's a goddamned idiot." He was trying to ease the tension, trying to sway my mood.

"You've been calling him a goddamned Idiot since you were kids." A sad smile formed when I accepted why Jacob hadn't shown up for his wedding day.

"Cora . . ." Matt's hand lowered over my back, his familiar warmth seeping into my skin. But something else was spreading inside, winding deeper. It was new, a remnant of what had resulted from our union last night.

I should have flinched away or slapped him or, hell, done a lot more, but I didn't. I couldn't. My life had just taken a direct flight to messed up, but for this one stolen moment, I was just going to pretend everything was fine. I was going to pretend that Matt had every right to touch me and I had every right to want him to touch me. Once this moment was done, I'd return to reality, but for right now . . . *fuck off, reality.*

"Last night, when you told me . . ." My throat felt like it was closing in on itself, so I had to swallow. "When you said you . . ."

I couldn't get it out. For some reason, I couldn't say those three words he'd uttered to me before, during, and after, each time, every time. Instead of torturing myself trying to get them out, I lifted my eyes to his. His eyes. Matt's eyes. God, what had I been thinking? They were so different from Jacob's. The emotions that tortured his were so different from the ones that toyed with Jacob's.

"Did you mean it?"

His jaw ground, but he didn't look away. He didn't blink. His eyes stayed on mine. As he was opening his mouth, something chimed between us. Call it divine intervention . . . in the form of a phone call.

"Shit. Sorry." Matt blew out a breath and shook his head like he was trying to shake himself out of a spell. When he pulled out his phone and glanced at the screen, his expression went dark.

"Who is it?" I asked, but I already knew.

Matt lifted the screen so I could see. I was right.

"What are you going to tell him?" That whimsical moment was gone, reality pouring over me.

"What do you want me to tell him?" He hit the silence on his ringer, waiting for me to answer. "What happened last night . . . if you don't want anyone to know, I swear I won't tell a soul. I'll take it to the grave. Just tell me what you want." His voice got tighter with each word as he searched my face for any hint of what to do next.

"Are you saying you'd be okay with lying to your own brother about the two of us sleeping together?" I scooted away from him, trying to ignore Jacob's second call coming in.

"I'm saying I'd be okay with anything if it's what you wanted."

When I wanted to cry from his words, I forced my eyes to narrow and my body to continue scooting away. "I want you to leave me alone. You had your chance to explain. You gave me your side of the story. Now leave me alone." I shoved to my feet, adjusting the sheet so it was still covering me. "I don't want you, Matt. I never have."

His face remained unaffected, but his eyes gave him away. The look in them made me feel like I was being ripped apart from the inside out. I was breaking him, one word at a time, and I hated myself more for what I was doing to Matt now than for how I'd betrayed Jacob last night.

"I want Jacob."

In the end, they say it's the lies we tell that define us more than the truths we admit. I already knew that. The lie I'd been telling for years had been defining me for just as long.

I loved Jacob. Not Matt.

That was the only version of myself I knew.

CHAPTER NINE

Matt

Just when a guy thought he might finally have a shot at the girl, she looked him point-blank in the eyes and told him she never had and never would want him. She wanted his brother. The same guy who was too busy getting a piece of ass to show up for his own damn wedding day.

Talk about a reality check. For a few minutes there when we'd been talking, I'd almost thought . . . I'd been foolish enough to hope . . . goddammit. I couldn't keep doing this to myself. Cora Matthews was my weakness. My addiction. Everything I wanted and everything I had to let go of.

I'd known that for years, but I hadn't accepted it until today. When I saw how broken she'd ended up as a result of what I'd done. When I realized how broken I was because of watching her fall in love with my brother.

I had to let her go. It wasn't a choice anymore, it was a requirement. Before we fucked up each other's lives any more than we already had.

Another call from Jacob popped up on my screen. If he wasn't already en route, he was about to be. It would be better to take his call now than wait until we were within arm's reach of each other and took out our emotions on each other's faces via our fists.

Cora had left a few minutes ago, having nothing else to say. She didn't want me—she wanted him. What else was there?

I didn't say anything when I finally answered his call.

I heard my brother suck in a breath. "Did you fuck her?"

My hand curled around the phone. He'd missed the wedding. He'd missed the whole entire day because he'd been screwing some girl he'd met in a bar. And me having sex with Cora was the first thing on his mind?

"You fucked her over enough all on your own." I didn't recognize my voice.

From the moment of silence on the other end, I guessed my brother didn't either. "You know what I mean, Matt."

Yeah, I did. And I wasn't going to tell him. Not until Cora made up her mind. If she wanted to tell him what had happened between us last night, I'd support that. If she didn't, I'd support that too. This wasn't about what I wanted to tell Jacob or what he wanted to know; this was about what Cora needed.

"Where were you?" I asked, rising from the crouched position I'd been in ever since she left. I couldn't kneel while having this conversation with my brother.

"None of your damn business where I was," he fired back. "Who the hell are you to think you could just slide into my spot when I wasn't looking?"

"It wasn't that you weren't looking. You were fucking some tramp when you should have been exchanging vows with your fiancée."

There was only the briefest beat of silence. "You don't know what I was doing. You don't know what happened."

"Yes, I do. Because you're you, and I'm me." My jaw locked when I pictured Jacob with someone else on Cora's and his wedding day. "Don't try to lie to me. I'm not like her, happy to overlook your faults."

"No, you're just happy to make your play for my girl when you saw the chance. You've been trying for years. You must have shit yourself when you saw your chance had finally arrived." From the sound of his voice, Jacob was drunk.

Trying to have a logical conversation with an illogical Jacob was a doomed endeavor.

"Do me a favor and call me back when you're sober. We can talk then." My thumb was hovering above the end button when Jacob laughed.

"I'll do you one better by showing up and talking to your face in a few hours. How about that?" Jacob let me process that for a few moments. "My plane's landing in St. Thomas at 3:25, so I'll see you soon. We can 'talk' this whole thing out. Oh, do me a favor and let Cora know, would you? For some reason, she doesn't seem to be answering her phone." The tone in Jacob's voice suggested exactly why she might not have been eager to answer his call.

I started heading back toward the cabin, needing to find Cora. If Jacob was going to be here in mere hours, I needed to find out what her plan was. I needed her to tell me what she wanted to admit to Jacob, if anything. As it was, already knew I'd posed as him for the wedding and reception, and he suspected that I'd kept with the theme into the wedding night.

"Good, I think we could all benefit from a 'talk.' Cora has a few questions as to where her fiancé was yesterday when he was supposed to be at his wedding." I gave him a moment to process that. "I have my suspicions, and so does she, but it will be nice to have it all cleared up once you get here."

"Matt—"

"Oh, and those Ass Clowns you call friends might have let a few things slip about your whereabouts when we were chatting at the reception when, you know, they thought I was you." I jogged down the beach, my emotions fueling my body.

"Matt—"

"Save it for later. When you have to look me in the eye and try to lie to me. When you have to look *her* in the eye and try to lie to her." It probably wouldn't make much of a difference to Jacob, because he'd been lying to Cora's face for years now. From small white lies to the grand-scale version such as where he was on their wedding day.

He might have been about to say something else, but I hung up. That phone conversation wasn't going anywhere—he had a reason to be pissed with me, and I had a reason to be pissed at him. No matter what we worked out on the phone, we'd have to work it out all over again when we came face-to-face. That was Jacob's and my way.

As soon as the cabin came into view, I knew she wasn't there. Whether it was that sixth sense or intuition, I knew I wouldn't find Cora inside. It didn't stop me from loping inside and checking though.

Housekeeping was there, trying to untangle the cyclone of sheets and blankets from last night. I didn't miss that Cora's purse and bags were missing. Even her clothes that had wound up scattered on the floor last night had been picked up and removed. It was like she'd vanished. Like she'd never even been here. With housekeeping making the bed and righting lamps that had tumbled over and cleaning bathroom mirrors that had been streaked with handprints, it was as though I'd made up all of last night.

God knew I'd pictured plenty of last nights in my head.

"The young woman? Did you see her?" I asked the two ladies cleaning the cabin.

They both avoided making eye contact, like they were afraid to answer me.

Finally, the one still wrestling with the sheets nodded. "She was here to get her bags."

I was pacing in circles, feeling like the whole world was going mad with myself leading the charge. "Did she mention where she was going?" I guessed the airport, either to meet Jacob when he arrived later or to catch her own plane out of here.

The woman focused extra intently on smoothing the sheet over the pillows.

"Please?" I added, not above getting on my knees and begging the woman if she had any idea where Cora had run off to. "I need to find her."

When she took a look at my face, she sighed. I must have looked really desperate. Good to know my expression matched the way I felt.

"The main hotel, sir," the woman answered. "She said she was checking into a room in the hotel."

At the same time I exhaled with relief, my heart kind of seized. She hadn't rushed to the airport as I'd expected, but she'd rushed to get out of this cabin and away from me. For her, last night had been a mistake, probably a moment she'd look back on and regret forever. But for me—pathetic, stupid me—last night had been the highlight of my existence, in this life and any and every other.

"Thank you," I said, fishing a couple of bills out of my wallet to leave as a tip before hurrying out the door.

She might not have wanted to see me, but too bad. She couldn't hide from this—she couldn't hide from me. What happened happened, and she could hate me to her dying breath if it made things easier for her, but I needed to know how she wanted to deal with Jacob. I needed to know what she was going to tell him so I knew what to expect. So I knew if the moment I saw him, I should start running because a moving target was harder to hit, or if I just needed to play it cool as the dutiful brother who'd stepped in to save the day and was stepping down now that the golden brother was back.

The path back to the hotel was a long one, but it didn't take more than a few minutes with the way I was running. My journey took me past the beach, and something caught my eye. I broke to a stop the moment I saw her. Tropical storm approaching or not, the beach was crowded with people. There was a little tiki bar toward the back, where people in brightly colored swimsuits were sipping brightly colored drinks. A few lines of lounge chairs accompanied striped umbrellas, and the thin swath of empty beach left over was fair game for people to sprawl out with their beach towels and toys.

In the middle of it all was Cora, in her basic white bikini, looking anything but ordinary. She was standing ankle-deep in the turquoise water, staring at the horizon like it was coming to get her. Dangling from one hand was a snorkel and in her other, a pair of fins. The water was calm and still, the storm having no effect on it yet, but she still surveyed the water like it was capable of growing fangs and coming for her.

Cora had never been particularly fond of the water. That had a lot to do with her learning to swim late in life. It seemed strange to me that, of all the things she could be doing right now, she was here, mustering up her courage as she took a few more steps into the water.

I had no idea if she'd already checked into a new room or why she was hanging at the beach when Jacob was hours away from descending on us both, but I didn't care. She was here. That was enough for me.

As I cut through the circus of beach towels and chairs, I couldn't help the smile I felt tugging at my mouth. She was trying to be so brave—I could tell from the way she was working her lip and almost looking as if she was staring down the ocean in front of her, like it was her nemesis. I also might have been smiling due to the way she looked in that bikini. Cora had a woman's body, curves instead of hard edges, and was more soft than she was firm. I loved that about her. I loved that she didn't feel the need to cover or disguise or diet her way down to fit into the size two clothes Jacob frequently bought her as a not-so-subtle hint.

Seeing her standing there in nothing more than a couple of scraps of fabric made my body ache as I remembered the way she'd felt against me. The way her skin felt sliding across my palm. The way her chest felt spilling against mine as I moved inside her. The way her lips felt moving down my throat.

And, great. Nothing like sporting a hard-on at a beach packed with people. Thankfully, no one seemed to be paying any special attention to the one person in pants and a button-down shirt instead of swimwear. I didn't miss the way plenty of people were noticing her though. I also didn't miss the way I wanted to crush their skulls from the looks they were giving her.

Shit. Talk about possessive. With a side of sick and twisted violent inclinations.

"Having one of those deep conversations with the Atlantic?"

She didn't flinch when she heard me behind her. She didn't even look surprised to see me there. "Less of a conversation and more of me trying to convince it I'm not terrified."

"How's that working out?"

Cora lifted the hand clutching a snorkel. It was trembling. "Not so great."

"Then why are you doing it?" I stepped into the water beside her after kicking off my shoes, not bothering to take the time to roll my pants up.

"Because I'm tired of being scared. I'm tired of feeling like I'm living my life based on fear, instead of standing from a point of strength." She sounded tired. She even looked tired. Neither of us had gotten much sleep last night, but this was a different kind of exhaustion. The kind that had been building for what looked like years.

"I heard you checked yourself into the hotel?" I matched her step when she journeyed farther into the water.

She nodded but didn't offer any kind of explanation. Not that she needed to. I knew why she had.

"Jacob's going to be here this afternoon. His flight arrives at 3:20." I watched her for a sign of any reaction, but all she did was acknowledge me with another nod, her eyes still focused on the vast body of water in front of us. "I need to know what you're planning on telling him. I'm behind you, whatever you decide, but I need to know because if he finds me first, I need to make sure our stories align." When her silence stretched on, I wound my hand around her wrist and angled myself slightly in front of her. "What do you want?"

Her eyes drifted to mine, the look in them making my throat tighten. She looked as lost as I'd ever seen a person, maybe even more lost than I felt at the present moment. Her throat moved when she swallowed. "I don't know, Matt. I don't know."

Her eyes looked like they were about to fill with tears, so I did what came naturally and wound my arms around her and tucked her close to me. She came into my embrace like it was exactly what she'd been waiting for, her head falling against my chest. Her back quaked a few times from what I guessed were stifled sobs, and we stood there just like that for a few minutes.

"It's going to be okay. I promise," I whispered, because it would be okay. I'd make sure it would be, even if I had to tell a million lies and sell my soul to keep that vow.

She nodded against my chest, almost like she believed me, but she didn't hurry to lean back or pull away. She seemed perfectly content to stay folded in my arms, standing knee-deep in the still ocean. I didn't realize it at first, but her body had stopped trembling in fear.

"What are you really doing?" I said.

"Trying to snorkel. Or at least working up the courage to try to snorkel."

"But you're scared of the water."

"And I'm tired of being scared of it. I told myself I was going to snorkel on my honeymoon, and I'm going to snorkel. I've always wanted to, and people do it everyday and live to tell the tale." She sniffed and leaned back, a brave expression plastered on her face.

"Plus, you're a strong swimmer. When you actually get in the water to swim."

The heaviness started to drain from her eyes. "Well, I did learn from the best."

I shrugged. "The *very* best."

She laughed, which made me wonder if she was thinking of the same memory I was. The first time I'd taken her to the country club pool when she was thirteen so I could give her her first swim lesson. I'd been on the swim team for years, so I thought I could teach her a thing or two. Except I forgot to account for how I felt whenever Cora was in a swimsuit. Especially when we were both in the water and I was trying to teach her how to back float, which meant touching, which meant my brain pretty much went into power-down mode.

"You told me it would only take a few lessons to teach me how to swim," she said, still laughing. "And it took a whole year of weekly lessons before I could finally make it a full lap without stopping."

I rubbed at the back of my head. "Practice makes perfect, right?"

"I don't know about perfect, but I've definitely had plenty of practice." She backed out of the water so she could sit on the sand and put on her fins. I guessed she was ready. "I can't believe you actually took the time once every week until we graduated to get in the water with me so I 'wouldn't forget what I'd learned.'"

I shifted so I was blocking the sun from her face. "I might have had ulterior motives for our weekly swim."

Her eyebrow lifted. "Pissing Jacob off?"

I shook my head, although those swim lessons had definitely pissed him off plenty.

She caught me staring at her and adjusted her top. "So you could see me in my swimsuit?"

I shook my head again, but I definitely hadn't minded seeing her in her swimsuit every week. I'd had to beat her into the water every time to try to disguise my "reaction" to seeing her in her swimsuit. And ten years later, same damn story, I thought as I slid my hand into my pocket.

"Because you were a good guy?" she said next.

Another head shake, because I wasn't a good guy. I was a far cry from that. "Because I wanted to be with you."

My answer took her a second to absorb. "In a chilly pool that you had to remind me how to do egg-beaters in every single week?"

I moved closer so my feet were between hers. "In the depths of hell roasting on a spit if it meant getting to be close to you."

Her chest stopped lifting with her breath, like I'd taken her by surprise. Which didn't make sense to me. Didn't she get it? Didn't she understand? Had I not been clear in my feelings for her?

Her breath returned, this time making her chest move extra fast. She was looking around like she was hoping for a distraction. "Will you go with me?"

"Yes," I answered, not knowing where or to do what, just knowing my answer was always yes where Cora was concerned.

Her shoulders seemed to sag with relief. "You can check out a mask and fins over there." She pointed at a bright white shed tucked back on the edge of the beach.

My fingers pinched the material of my slacks. "I don't have a swimsuit. I'll have to go back to the cabin first."

Her head shook as she scanned the beach. "I need to go now or else I'll chicken out." Her eyes widened on something before she pointed down the beach again. "There. You can just buy one and change into it."

My gaze followed the direction she was pointing in, and my mouth fell into a frown. A vendor was carrying what looked like an umbrella lined with an endless supply of bright colors and wild prints. "Those are women's swimsuits."

From the corner of my eyes, I noticed her shake her head. "They're men's swimsuits." She was already waving over the vendor. "European-cut men's swimsuits."

"Banana hammocks." My hand thrust in the direction of the "swimwear" swishing toward us. "You're suggesting I put on a banana hammock and strut around on a beach filled with children and old women?"

The vendor was already lowering the curtain hanging around his mobile umbrella shop. The privacy seemed kind of ironic, since I'd be emerging from said changing room dressed in a swimsuit that was basically Lycra dental floss.

Cora shrugged like the answer was obvious.

"Why do you think I'm going to do this?"

She smiled at me, her light eyes finding mine. "Because you get to be with me?"

CHAPTER TEN

Cora

He really would do anything to be with me. He actually meant it.

When I'd suggested the Speedo store on wheels, I hadn't actually expected him to go for it. I'd expected him to head back to the cabin, change into his swim trunks, then meet me back here. He hadn't though. He was behind that circular curtain now, stripping down and actually putting on one of those things.

I wasn't sure what to make of it. I wasn't sure what to make of him. He was saying things, doing things that seemed totally out-of-character. Matt had been so standoffish and distant with me for so long, but he'd been the opposite over the past two days. He'd been the Matt I remembered falling for as a young girl, instead of the Matt I'd come to know ever since Jacob and I got together.

God, Jacob. He was coming. I could ignore his calls and try to pretend he wouldn't be here this afternoon, but that didn't change that he *would* be standing in front of me today, asking some hard questions. I should have been focusing on what I was going to say to him. I should have been barred inside the room I'd just checked into and crying myself senseless over the mess I'd found myself in. I should have been trying to drown Matt for what he'd done and how he'd deceived me, instead of asking him to go snorkeling with me like this was our honeymoon.

I was such a wreck, such a ball of confusion, and I didn't know what to think or do. My head was pulling me in one direction, and my gut was pulling me in the other. I couldn't have both, I'd always known that, but now, I wasn't even sure if I was entitled to one of them.

Because I might not have known I was making love to Matt last night, but that certainly hadn't stopped me from wishing it would happen again. How could I look Jacob in the eye ever again after being with his brother last night? How could I look Matt in the eye ever again after being with his brother for years?

It was an impossible situation, so I did the only thing I could and shut it out. I ignored it, knowing it wouldn't go away, but I was content to set it aside temporarily.

"Did you pick one yet?" Matt hollered from the mobile changing room.

"I thought you did." I stood and dusted the sand off my backside, trying not to stare at Matt's slacks that had just fallen around his ankles.

"I'm going to leave that honor up to you. I want it on record that I had no say in any of this when it comes back to bite me in the ass."

I shifted through a few selections hanging from the top of the umbrella. I still couldn't believe he was actually doing this.

"Do you have anything against animal print?" I winked at the vendor when I came across a flashy python print.

"I have a thing against dressing like a male stripper in public."

"So you're saying you're a fan of animal print?" I'd already unclipped the python one from the ring.

"Just give me the damn thing already? I'm standing here naked, and if a strong breeze comes along, I'm about to give the whole beach a free show."

I tossed my selection over the top of the curtain while he kicked his wallet out at my feet.

"You're evil," he said, followed by a drawn-out groan. "I'm not wearing this."

"Too late. Already paid for." I handed the twenty to the vendor, who pocketed it so quickly it was like he was worried we'd change our minds.

"Not doing it."

"Stop being a baby, Matt. It's just a swimsuit."

He huffed over the swimsuit part. "All I need is a shaver and some body oil and I could star in some low-budget porn."

That made me laugh, which made him laugh.

"Come on. Pick me out something else. A solid or something less . . . *snaky.*"

"You asked me to pick, and that's what I picked. 'No returns, refunds, or exchanges,'" I said, pretending I was reading some sign hanging off the vendor's money apron.

"The only way I'm putting this thing on is if someone holds me down and forces me into it. No way am I tugging this thing on of my own volition."

My eyes lifted, and before I knew what I was doing, I was slipping through the curtain. Matt looked as surprised by me as I was by him. I'd forgotten that he was naked. Fully. The same fully naked way he'd been last night when he'd done things to me I'd never had done before.

The same things I was thinking about right now, which was making my body respond in ways that were not family-beach appropriate.

I had to clear my throat before I could say anything. "You were saying?"

It was tight quarters in here, and Matt had no issue making them tighter as he stepped into me. His eyes darkened when he felt my chest brush against his, not missing the way my mouth parted from the way I was breathing.

"The only way I'm wearing that is if you hold me down . . ." His mouth lowered so it was outside my ear. "And force me."

When his warm breath fogged across my neck, I shivered. He didn't miss it, as confirmed by the way one corner of his mouth lifted. He'd barely touched me and my body was already responding. We were in some small mobile changing room on a packed beach, and I could feel my body making itself ready for him, like all he had to do was say the word and I'd do his every bidding.

"So unless you have any reason for wanting to keep me in my birthday suit . . ." His gaze dropped to the sand, where the scrap of Lycra was waiting.

"And here I'd been under the impression all these years you were the chivalrous type."

I felt his smile aimed at me as I kneeled. "A chivalrous man is not the same as a perfect man."

"Clearly," I muttered, trying to focus on what I was doing instead of who I was doing it to, and how said person was bare-ass naked.

Grabbing the python scrap of fabric, I held it by his feet and waited. I didn't dare look up because I was worried it wouldn't be his eyes I'd connect with. Not at this level. And then I didn't trust what would happen next.

Which was so inappropriate to think or fantasize about, given we were on a public beach and my real fiancé was en route as I kneeled in front of his naked twin, my swimsuit bottoms damp from something other than a morning swim.

"This was a good idea," Matt said, his tone amused. "A *great* idea," he added as I pulled the scrap of fabric up over his knees.

They were going to be tight, I discovered after having to practically wrestle them up his thighs. I'd almost tugged the python wonder into place when . . .

"Oh my god, Matt!" I half-shrieked, but I didn't even try to divert my eyes. If he didn't have any shame over his "issue," I wouldn't have any over my staring issue.

"I'm naked and standing in front of a beautiful woman while she dresses me. And this isn't supposed to turn me on how?"

I didn't miss the way his jaw ground when I finished yanking the swimsuit into place. Now that I was standing in front of him, he couldn't look at me. I wondered why. He was trying to be playful and make it seem like this whole thing was a fun joke, but I could tell he was holding himself back. From saying something or doing something, I wasn't sure, but he wasn't half as relaxed and at ease as he was trying to convince me he was.

When I glanced down, I had to bite my cheek to keep from laughing. The swimsuit was impossibly small, hardly able to cover his package . . . especially when it was at full staff. The back was the same story. More of his ass hung out than was covered.

"Looks like we should have gone with the extra-large for you," I said at last, having to cover my mouth when a laugh wanted to follow. He looked ridiculous.

Matt winked, his eyes lowering to his groin. "Glad you noticed."

Rolling my eyes, I gave him a shove before ducking out of the dressing area. I figured I'd give him a minute to gather his courage before stepping out in his special new swimsuit. I headed to the rental shack to check out another snorkel set. When the employee asked for Matt's shoe size so he could get the right size fins, I realized I could immediately remember what size Matt's feet were. I couldn't remember Jacob's the same way. It was there—size twelve compared to Matt's size thirteen—but the knowledge wasn't instant, burned into my memory like all things Matt were.

Like the way he liked his toast practically burned to a crisp or how he tapped his left index finger whenever he'd been studying for a hard test or the way his arm would whip out in front of whoever was in the passenger seat when he was driving and had to slam the brakes. Matt was committed to my memory, the way a person recalled their birthday.

By the time I'd made it back from the rental shack, Matt had emerged from the dressing room and was drawing no shortage of attention. The suit was insanely tight, but if anyone could wear a so-called banana hammock, Matt Adams was that person.

With the sun beating down on him, his skin glowing from what I guessed was perspiration . . . damn, he looked good. Too good.

I made myself look away when he glanced my way. I was confused enough about how I felt for Matt and how he felt in return; I didn't need to confuse him any more by giving him lingering looks.

We had enough complications to sort through.

So wasn't this just the ideal time to go snorkeling? My subconscious laughed at me as I held out the extra snorkel set for Matt. *You've just slept with the wrong man after marrying him, and your fiancé is on the way to find out what the hell is going on. Snorkeling is the obvious answer to that conundrum, right?*

"Ready?" Matt had already slipped on his fins and mask and was backing into the water.

As I followed his lead, I didn't find the same panic waiting for me. I'd never gone above my head in the ocean. Actually, I'd never even gone past my waist. The pool was different, safer somehow, but this was the ocean. It seemed endless and unpredictable.

"You look good in that thing, you know?"

He huffed. "No, I really don't. But it's good to be with you, so that's enough for me." His gaze went all-intentional on me again as we treaded into the deeper water.

I didn't realize I was treading water, making my eggbeaters all on my own without needing a refresher first. I was doing it. On my own. Because of him.

"Is that the truth?" I asked, swimming closer to him. "Is just being with me—around me—good enough for you?"

I wasn't sure if he'd understand the meaning behind my words. From the look on his face as he slid the mask back on his head, I knew he had. "No." He didn't blink. "It isn't good enough. But it will have to do."

CHAPTER ELEVEN

Matt

What was she feeling? What was she thinking?

One minute I thought I knew, and the next I didn't have a damn clue. I knew she wasn't purposefully trying to send me mixed signals, but I'd never felt so confused in my goddamned life. One second she was looking at me in *that* way, saying things, doing things . . . and the next she was turning her back and glancing at me like I was just another one of the seven billion occupants of the planet.

The snorkeling thing had been unexpected. Awesome, but not exactly what I thought I'd find her doing an hour after finding out about what I'd done, and hours before Jacob would be here. Maybe that was why she was acting so all over the place—because she was in shock or something. God knew people had been traumatized by less.

She still hadn't brought up anything about Jacob or what she wanted to tell him. It was just past noon, which meant we had a few hours to decide how we were going to play this. The ball was in her court, and I'd play the game by her rules. Once I found out what those rules were.

"That was fun," she said as we plodded into the hotel with dripping hair and salty skin. She'd asked me if I'd walk her in, and like the hopeless sucker I was for her, of course I said yes.

Okay, so she still wasn't ready to talk about Jacob. Not that I was in a hurry either.

"You did good out there. You're a strong swimmer."

"I did learn from the best." She smiled at me, her eyes dropping to where I'd cinched a beach towel tightly around my new beach attire. "Though for a swimmer, I wouldn't have thought you'd be so squeamish about wearing a Speedo."

I nudged her as I walked her toward the elevators. "A Speedo is what one wears for swimming practice or an event. It contains more fabric, offers more coverage, and doesn't typically come in python print. This"—I motioned at the area below my navel—"is what one wears when auditioning for Snake on Snake Action."

When she laughed, it spread throughout the whole foyer. Man, that laugh. Cora used to laugh like that a lot when we were kids, but things had changed. Now her laughs were more of the measured, rehearsed variety.

When we made it to the row of elevators, she didn't hit the up button. She looked like she was struggling to say something, and I guessed I knew what it had to do with.

"If you want, you can call me later when you decide," I said, leaning into the wall in front of her. "I'll keep my phone on me, so just let me know what you want to tell Jacob." I patted the pocket of my slacks bunched in my arm and waited.

I knew it was time for me to leave, but I wasn't ready. Something inside me knew that when I left Cora this time, it might be months before I saw her again. Maybe years. That was how I guessed it would have to be for her to put the last twenty-four hours behind her. She might have been content for the last couple of hours to forget about what I'd done, but I knew that wouldn't last. Her anger would come back, evolve into disgust, transition into loathing, and turn into god only knew what before hopefully, one day, she'd be able to look at me and remember me for the person I'd been the thousands of days before this past one.

"Would you come up with me?" she asked quietly, like she was afraid of saying it too loudly. "Would you mind walking me to my room?"

No. Say no, Matt. You don't need to fuck this up any more than you've already fucked it.

"Sure." The word was out of my mouth instantly, my palm already pressing into the up button.

At the same time Cora looked relieved, she appeared just as shocked.

We didn't say anything on the elevator ride up. I noticed that she hadn't gone with the penthouse like Jacob had originally planned. Instead, the elevator stopped somewhere in the middle of the tall tower. As we moved down the hall, I felt hyperaware of every wet strand of hair winding down her back, every freckle dotted across her shoulders, every breath she seemed to labor over.

When she stopped in front of a door, she dug a card key out of her beach bag and struggled to get it slid in and out with the way her hand was trembling.

"Let me." I took the card from her and unlocked the door. When I held the card out for her as she stepped into the room, I realized she was crying. Or she was about to. I slid her hair away from her face so I could see her eyes better. "Cora?"

When her eyes lifted to mine, the first tear rolled down her cheek. "I'm scared."

A lump lodged in my throat from seeing her like this, hearing those words come from her. "What are you scared of?"

I had a few guesses, of course, but I wanted to hear it from her.

When she shook her head and sealed her lips, I stepped closer. "Afraid of what Jacob's going to do? Afraid of what he'll say?"

Her eyes stayed closed as a few more tears chased down her cheeks. "Yeah, I guess I'm nervous about Jacob and what's going to happen when we see each other this afternoon."

My brows pulled together. What else besides Jacob was she scared of? "Anything else?"

She was quiet for such a stretch of time that I didn't think she was going to answer me. Then her eyes opened, and she forced them to meet mine. "I'm scared of you." She looked like she was working up a measure of courage to say whatever she needed to next.

"Scared of me?" My head shook because I didn't understand. She had nothing to be scared of when it came to me. Whatever she needed from me, whatever lies she needed me to corroborate, whatever truths she needed me to bury, I was hers.

She sucked in a breath. "I'm scared of the feelings I have for you."

An impact. That was the sensation I felt upon hearing those words come from her. Harmless words were somehow capable of making me feel like I'd just been wrecked and gutted at the same time.

They weren't just any words. They were the very ones I'd been waiting to hear from her for years. She had some kind of feelings for me.

"What kind of feelings?" I rasped, knowing better than to hope. I had a decade of experience proving why hope was pointless where Cora and I were concerned.

"You know what kind of feelings," she whispered.

Shit, Matt. Do the right thing. The right thing . . .

What the fuck is the right thing?

"Just stop and think about what you're saying for a minute. The past couple of days have been . . . a lot's happened." I was trying to put my thoughts together, but none of the pieces seemed to fit. I knew what I had to say, but it was the opposite of how I felt. The result was me sounding like a blundering idiot. "Yesterday, the things I did, I did in the heat of the moment. Maybe if I'd stopped to think, paused to question if I was doing the right thing, none of this would have happened. You wouldn't be in the situation you are right now."

Cora's hand had slipped into mine, and she was guiding me into her room. I didn't realize I'd let go of the door until I heard it slam closed.

"Instead I'd be in the situation of being humiliated in front of hundreds of guests at the wedding my fiancé failed to show up to? The situation of being alone and sad and scared?"

"But you're scared right now," I argued, reminding myself why I had to do the right thing when it came to Cora.

"Have you ever noticed how the more you do or admit or talk about whatever it is that scares you, the less it actually does?" The card key fell out of my hand when Cora's other hand molded around my shoulder. "Like today, I was terrified to get in that water and snorkel, but once I decided I was going to do it no matter what, once I started to, I wasn't scared anymore. I felt brave instead."

My heart was hammering against my sternum, echoing in my eardrums. I nodded.

"I'm tired of being scared. I want to be brave, not frightened." She moved closer, until the cloth from her towel was scratching against my chest. Her eyes dropped to my mouth. "Be brave with me."

The right thing.

Do the right thing.

That was the chant going through my head when her mouth covered mine, her arms winding around my neck as she fitted her body against mine.

Whatever the right thing was, I couldn't remember it, especially with the way she was kissing me. But this felt pretty damn right.

Fuck it.

I'd already made love to her four times in a day. What was once more?

"We have to talk," I managed to get out.

"We will," she whispered against my lips. "I promise. We'll talk about everything. Until we've figured it all out."

My mouth responded, claiming hers with my tongue, drawing a sound from deep inside her. My hands formed around her backside, lifting her off of the ground so her legs could tangle around me. When our laps collided, I rocked myself into her, desperate for her to feel my need for her. Desperate for her to know the depth of my need was as limitless as my love for her was.

"Matt," she breathed against my mouth, making every nerve in my body come alive.

"Say it again." I leaned back so I could watch my name form on her lips.

Her back bowed when I pressed myself against her again, my fingers digging deeper into her backside.

"Matt," she breathed once more, her eyes meeting mine as she pitched against me.

I couldn't wait. As much as I wanted to prolong this and draw it out into the next decade, I couldn't wait.

"Next time you say it, I'm going to be inside you." Grabbing her towel, I yanked it free and tossed it onto the floor. She worked at my towel, slipping her hand inside to stroke me a few times. "Wait, I'm too close. I need to be inside you. I need to feel you when I come."

Cora reached between us and slid aside the material of her swimsuit. A moment later, she freed me from the confines of my own suit. She pressed herself against me, sliding up and down my aching length so I could feel how ready she was to take me. How much she wanted me.

Me. Matt.

Not Jacob.

Not me pretending to be Jacob.

Me.

Matt Adams.

The man who'd loved her for so long, I couldn't remember a time when I hadn't. Loving her had become a part of me. The defining part of me.

"Matt," she sighed, her hands curling into fists. "Please."

Hearing my name, listening to her practically beg—I knew better, but I couldn't do better. Not with Cora. Not when it was her asking something of me. This, perhaps more than anything else, proved why I was so weak where she was concerned.

Shoving off the wall, I moved until my knees hit the mattress. Caging my arms around her back, I lowered her onto the bed, crashing my mouth into hers the moment her head hit the pillow. With her help, I finished tearing out of that god-awful swimsuit and kicked it to the floor. When I ground myself between her legs, her head rolled back, her mouth fell open, and a sound that drove me wild tumbled from her lips.

I was making her feel those things. Responsible for the sounds she was making for me. God, acknowledging that made me feel drunk with power.

"Please, Matt," she whimpered again, shimmying out of her swimsuit bottoms.

"Don't stop saying my name." My jaw ground when she slid aside her top, revealing her breasts. "Don't stop saying it."

She nodded, biting her lip as I continued to rock my hips into her, trying to hold off for one last moment before I took her. I knew once I felt her, it would all be over. I probably should have been embarrassed by how quickly I came whenever I sank into her, but I wasn't. Not the slightest bit of shame. She was everything I'd ever dreamed of, my proverbial fantasy in human form.

My mouth skimmed down her neck, my tongue leaving a wet trail. She arched closer the lower I went, and when I got to the heavy crest of her breast, I couldn't help myself. I sucked on her skin hard, desperate to mark this exact spot on her body. Desperate to mark every spot of her body.

"Matt," she whimpered, squirming as I worked at that perfect patch of skin.

When I pulled back, I grinned at what I'd done. Inside, my inner animal roared. A large red mark was starting to blossom at the top of her breast, and it looked so fucking perfect on her, I wanted to give the other one a mark to match.

Before I got there, the hotel phone rang. Below me, Cora jolted like she'd just been shaken out of a dream.

"It's okay. Let it ring." My mouth dropped to her neck again, loving the taste of the salty ocean on her skin.

"The front desk said they'd call to check to make sure I liked my room, or find out if I'd want to move."

"The front desk can wait." My fingers scrolled down her side, making her shiver. Between my legs, a growing ache was building. I wasn't sure I could delay much longer.

"It'll only take a second." She smiled at me as she shimmied over to where the phone was ringing on the nightstand. "Overeager much?"

"Where you're concerned?" My brow lifted. "Overeager always."

She laughed softly then lifted her index finger as she grabbed the phone. While she did that, I reached between my legs to give my balls a squeeze because damn, they were not known for their patience.

"Hello?" she said, trying to sound natural, but she sounded breathless and excited, like she'd totally been getting laid. Or about to.

Immediately, her face went blank. And white. Her body froze at the same time.

"Jacob?" She swallowed, her eyes connecting with mine for one beat before she looked away.

My heart had managed to lodge itself in my throat when I heard her say his name. There I was, naked and hovering above his girl, while he was on the other end of the phone with her.

This was seriously messed up.

"Yeah, Matt found me. He told me you're flying in later." Her lips moved, but that was all. Everything else looked paralyzed in fear. Or something like it.

I wanted her to shake her head when I crawled off of her. I wanted her hand to reach for mine when I pulled away. I wanted her to drape her arms around me again and hold me close, so I knew. So I knew she wanted me to stay. She wanted me close.

But she didn't want me close. She didn't want me to stay. She didn't make any move to stop me when I lifted away from her and crawled off of the bed.

"No, I'm in another room. Not the penthouse, no—" Cora sat up in bed, throwing the downy comforter over her body like we were a couple of kids again and I'd accidently walked in on her changing or something. "Listen, Jacob, a lot has happened, and I'm not going to sit here and explain it all to you over the phone—"

He must have cut her off again. Jacob had been cutting her off and interrupting her forever. For some reason, this time, I wanted to figure out a way to reach through that phone and wrap my hands around his neck.

Things had changed between Cora and me. We'd slept together. We'd shared things. I might not have had any claim to her, but I wanted one. I wanted to be able to say she was my girl and use whatever means necessary to protect her, even if it meant driving my fist into my brother's jaw if he kept interrupting her and using that raised voice I could hear from across the room.

"I'm not having this conversation with you right now. I'm not doing it." Cora seemed to have forgotten about me completely.

I was plenty used to that. When Jacob was involved, I was there one minute, invisible the next.

I was such a fool. Such a goddamn idiot.

She didn't want me. She wanted him. She always had and nothing was going to change that—least of all me confessing the way I felt about her.

Anger seeped into my blood, making me feel like I could tear apart this entire hotel, one crumbled fistful at a time. I tuned out whatever Cora was saying as I snagged one of the towels off the floor and cinched it back around my waist.

She never looked up. Her attention never diverted from the phone and who was on the other end of it.

As I started for the door, something stopped me. Exhaling, I turned so I was facing her, waiting for a chance to get her attention. It didn't take as long as I expected.

When her eyes connected with mine, I saw a dozen emotions playing in them. She was scared, nervous, unsure. At the same time, she looked relieved, happy, and almost peaceful.

"Are you okay?" I mouthed, waiting. I couldn't leave her if she needed me, but there had been few times in life when Cora had needed me over Jacob. I hoped this might be one of those times, but I knew it wasn't.

She took a moment, her throat moving when she swallowed. Then she pulled the covers tighter around her and nodded. After that, her gaze left me and her whole focus shifted back to the phone. Even from here, I could still hear Jacob's raised voice as he fired questions and accusations at her, pausing half a second before popping off the next.

What did she see in my brother? What did she see in him that she didn't when she looked at me?

I guessed the answer to that was everything, because Jacob was everything I wasn't, just like I was everything he wasn't. We were twins, two halves of what had started as a whole, but life and experience had turned us into totally different people.

As I pulled the door open, I heard Cora get in a few words. "Okay, yeah. I'll see you soon." A pause, just long enough for my heart to feel as though it were turning to stone. "I love you too."

CHAPTER TWELVE

Matt

What had driven me to this? Sitting here, perched on the sidewalk curb, staring through the hotel windows at some girl waiting for another man?

I'd been camped here for the past hour, as long as she'd been stationed in that chair in the lobby. Both of us were waiting for a cab to roll up carrying Jacob. It was almost seven, which meant his flight had been delayed . . . or he'd been delayed in one of the airport bars. Which tended to happen frequently.

He'd had a drinking problem for years, and Cora had seemed content to overlook it. That was the only answer, because I knew she was aware of it. She wasn't stupid and she wasn't naïve; she knew Jacob's problem, but she accepted it. If that was what you wanted to call it.

She had on another pretty dress, this one cobalt blue and providing more coverage than the one she'd worn on the flight yesterday.

Cora couldn't see me—it was dark outside and I was a couple hundred feet back—but I could see her. She'd been waiting for him as long as I had, pulling her phone out of her purse every few minutes to check it. She'd been nursing the same glass of wine for the past hour and had barely finished half of it. Even from back here, I could tell she was nervous—she kept shifting in her seat, crossing her legs, uncrossing them, crossing her ankles, fidgeting with her hands in her lap. She looked like she'd never been so uncomfortable, and even though I shouldn't have cared how she felt after what had happened this afternoon, I did. Staying where I was, watching her through a plate of glass, when she was so distressed went against my every instinct.

Every time I felt the muscles in my legs twitch, ready to get up and go to her, I put myself back in her hotel room and remembered the way she'd gone from whispering my name and sharing her body with me, to completely ignoring me when Jacob's call came in. How could a person who'd just looked at me like I was special act like I wasn't even in the room sixty seconds later?

I'd never thought Cora could do that until today. But now I knew, because what other explanation was there? She'd had a temporary use for me—forgetting herself and what had happened—but once Jacob came back into the picture, her need for me was gone.

We hadn't gotten to have that talk I'd planned on—the one about what she wanted to tell Jacob when he showed up. We didn't need to though, because I already knew what story she would weave for him. The one he wanted to hear. The one that would be easiest to admit. The one that was a lie.

Cabs had been scooting through the circular entrance of the hotel all night, though most of them were leaving with guests headed for the airport, thanks to the tropical storm still making its way in this direction. No one working at the hotel seemed too concerned about it, and growing up in Miami, I had enough experience with hurricanes to not let the possibility of a tropical storm get to me. However, it was obvious plenty of other vacationers weren't so copacetic with the weather forecast.

When a cab pulled up with someone in the backseat, I knew it was him. It was that twin sense, I guessed, the one that came from sharing a womb for nine months and every milestone in life since.

Jacob was here.

He was my brother, and I loved him, and I wanted him to have a good and happy life—I really did—but right then, seeing him crawl out of that cab, his gaze falling on the same woman I'd been staring at for the past hour . . . I kind of wanted to beat his ass right there on the sidewalk.

After paying the cabbie, he slung a small duffel bag over his shoulder and started up the stairs toward the lobby. He wasn't staggering, but he was moving just slowly enough to give away that he'd been drinking. When he swayed as he reached the landing, I guessed he'd drank enough to be considered drunk by driving standards, but barely buzzed by Jacob's.

When he moved through the sliding glass doors, he took a moment to scan the lobby like he didn't have a fucking clue where she was. When he damn well did. The blood in my veins heated again. Jacob had been doing that to Cora forever, acting like he wasn't as under her spell as I knew he was. Like he didn't have a clue where she was at a party or what she was doing or who she was talking to. He did. He always did, but he didn't want her to know it. He didn't want her to know just how much he felt for her.

So, there. I guess there was one way my brother and I were alike—in our apprehension to make our true feelings known for the same woman.

Cora noticed him right away, rising out of her chair so quickly, it scooted back a few inches. She didn't know what to do with her hands, and if she didn't stop twisting them together, he would know something was wrong.

Like she'd had the same thought I had, her hands fell to her sides and she calmed her body. She opened her mouth, probably calling his name, before moving toward where he was still standing at the front doors, looking around like a dipshit.

He turned toward her after that, but I couldn't make out the look on his face. They were some distance away and turned to the side, so I couldn't tell if that was a smile or a frown on his face. With Cora, I could tell. She was smiling. At least the contrived version. She was nervous, and she had every right to be. The man she'd promised to marry had shown up on the same island where she and the twin she'd accidently married had spent the last twenty-four hours.

No wonder Jacob had sounded so anxious earlier. He had every right to be, although I knew Cora would do everything she could to convince him nothing had happened. Other than, you know, her and I exchanging vows and posing as husband and wife in front of hundreds of his friends and colleagues. That was enough to send Jacob through the roof without finding out about what else had happened.

Jacob started toward her, both of them moving toward each other until only a few steps separated them. They both rolled to a stop, Cora being the first to freeze. That, I hadn't been expecting. I'd imagined her throwing herself into his arms, listing off a litany of apologies, then the two of them would go ride off into the gray and stormy sunset.

Not quite.

Jacob stood there, waiting for a moment, then he said something. I couldn't read lips, and I couldn't begin to imagine what my brother would think to say to the woman he'd pretty much left at the altar when he saw her for the first time.

Why was Cora looking like the only guilty one when Jacob had a shitload more guilt than she ever could?

He said something else, his arms going out at his sides. She was quiet, listening to him speak. He wasn't yelling, like I'd expected. That might have been part of the reason I was hanging where I was, in case I needed to intervene if he flew off the cuff like Jacob had been known to do. I'd had to tear him off a guy at a college party once when he'd caught him checking out Cora's ass. He'd practically turned the guy's face into a science experiment, only to find out later that the guy was gay. If he had been looking in Cora's ass's general direction, he'd probably been coveting her designer jeans.

If Jacob found out what his own brother had done with Cora, he'd probably try to kill me. Which, at this present moment, I was good with. I wanted to kill myself for the way I'd let things get out of control.

Jacob kept talking, his hands and arms moving in sync with whatever he was saying. The whole time, Cora stayed still and quiet, listening. When he finished, he shrugged. Had he just told her why he'd missed the wedding? Had he just admitted what he'd been doing and who he'd been doing it with? From the way Cora was still standing there, I didn't think so, but what else could he have said that took five minutes to get out?

After a moment, he opened his arms and waited. Cora didn't go into them instantly, the way I'd seen her do before. She waited, staring at him like she was debating her next move. What was she thinking? What was going through her mind? Was I anywhere in there? Was I any part of the reason for her standing her ground when Jacob wanted her to come to him?

A moment later, I had my answer. She went from frozen to flying, practically throwing herself against him as she tucked her head below his and wound her arms behind him. Jacob's arms came around her, his lips dropping to her head. He was touching her, kissing her. His hands were touching the same places I had earlier. His lips were brushing the same places mine had.

God, my jealousy was a living, breathing thing right then. I'd felt no shortage of it in my life—we'd been on a first-name basis for a while—but I'd never felt it like this. Like it was alive and capable of consuming me if I let it.

Why was I still sitting there? Why was I watching this happen?

Enough, Matt. Fucking enough.

Shoving up from the sidewalk, I glanced around, lost for what to do next, where to go. My whole life felt like it was gone, eradicated in a twenty-four hour period. Before I could move, I watched my brother's mouth lower to her ear and whisper something that made her nod. Then he guided her out of the lobby, toward the row of elevators. I didn't leave until I watched the up button light up. I didn't leave until I watched them climb onto the next elevator that opened for them. I didn't leave until I watched the woman I loved head up to her room with my twin brother.

The damn story of my life.

Me waiting and watching while she left with him. Me loving her every second of every day while she gave her love to him. Me willing to give anything I had for her when she didn't want anything from me.

I needed to get off this island. Tonight. Even if it meant buying a boat and rowing my ass back to the mainland, I was leaving. I couldn't stay. I'd finally accepted that Cora would never choose me.

But first, I needed a drink. One that would hopefully dull the images and emotions coursing through me right now.

I'd seen a little beach bar earlier when we went snorkeling, so that was where I headed. I knew there were plenty of places to get a drink inside the hotel, but I wasn't stepping foot in there. Especially not with what I knew was about to happen, if not already happening, eight floors up.

As I stormed across the grounds, I couldn't let myself think about her. Every time an image of her flashed into my mind, I set a match to it. Every time I remembered the sounds I'd driven from her or the way her hands felt moving across me or the way her eyes had looked into mine while I moved above her, I doused them in imaginary kerosene and set fire to each and every one.

I'd wasted years waiting for her. Decades. I wasn't about to waste one more fucking minute of my life on someone who didn't give a damn about me.

The bar was fairly quiet when I got there. Only one couple, who looked like locals, was pressed against each other as they sipped on their beers. The bartender took one look at my face and immediately lined up a few bottles on the counter. I pointed at the first one in the lineup, not knowing what it was and not giving a shit either.

"How do you want it?" the bartender asked as he put back the other bottles.

"In a glass," I said, sliding onto the first stool I came to.

The bartender nodded like he understood, reaching for a glass and pouring whatever brand of poison I'd pointed at. I wasn't sure. I'd never been a big drinker—my twin had more than made up for my restraint in that area.

Of course, after watching him turn to the bottle whenever life got tough, I should have known better than to do the same when my own life got fucking destroyed, but I'd played nice my whole life and look where it had gotten me. Nowhere. The good guy hadn't gotten the girl, so to hell with that.

The moment I lifted the glass to my lips, I cringed from the fumes alone. I guessed this wasn't the type of drink a person sipped and enjoyed—better to just get it down so it could get me good and drunk.

Tipping my head back, I drained the glass in one long swallow. My throat felt like it was on fire and my tongue felt like the top layer of skin had been boiled off, but I could already feel the drink's warmth spreading into my veins. But just in case . . .

"I'll have one more," I said, setting the glass on the lacquered wood counter.

The bartender gave me a look that read *Do you need to talk?* I answered with one hard shake of my head.

No, I didn't want to talk. I wanted to drink. I wanted to get shit-faced so I could forget about her for one damn hour of my life.

I was just about to lift my second glass of battery acid to my lips when I noticed someone slide onto a stool a couple down from me. It was a woman, but it wasn't *the* woman, so I kept my focus on my drink. That was the way it had always been—Cora, and everyone else. I'd been so consumed by her, I'd failed to notice anyone else. What if, because of my fixation, I'd let the right one slip away? What if I'd let a whole stream of right ones get away, all because I'd been consumed by the wrong one?

That thought made the second drink go down easier. And quicker.

"If it wasn't for that look of remorse in your eyes, I would have thought you were Jacob after watching you take down that liter of vodka."

Her voice was familiar, but it wasn't a voice I was expecting to hear right now, on this island, feet away from where I was attempting to drink myself into a stupor. Twisting on my stool, I had to blink a couple of times to make sure I was really seeing who I thought I was. The booze was already messing with my senses, making my head feel like it was stuffed with cotton.

"Maggie?" My forehead creased. "Is that you?"

The woman sitting two stools over gave me a look that suggested I was a moron—which I supposed was dead-on. "No. It's me, the Ghost of Maggie Future."

Huffing, I slid my empty glass toward the bartender again. "Now I know you're you. Nobody can make me feel like a bigger idiot than Maggie Stevenson."

"Really? After the past two days, it seems like you've taken over that role."

When the bartender wasn't as quick to fill my glass this time, I lifted it and shook it a few times, trying to catch his attention. He was a little distracted by a pair of brunettes who had just slid up to the bar in dresses that were pretty much a second skin.

"You can't make an idiot out of someone when they're already one. And that's been my birthright from the very start. Sorry."

Since the bartender didn't look like he was going to be making his way over here any time soon, I leaned over the counter, grabbed the bottle, and attempted to pour it into my glass.

Maggie huffed when she watched me spill more of the vodka onto the bar than into my actual glass. "I think you hit your limit one and a half glasses ago. Slow down."

My head shook as I kept pouring. "My limit tonight is when I pass out. After that, you have my word I'll stop drinking."

"Something to look forward to," she muttered.

"By the way, what in the hell are you doing here?" Instead of setting the bottle back behind the counter, I kept it in arm's reach. For when I needed a refill. Or five.

"Ah, I was wondering when you might get around to wondering that." Maggie's eyebrow lifted as she slid a few curls behind her ear. "Imagine my surprise when I heard you didn't make it to your brother's wedding because you'd gotten food poisoning, but when I showed up at your condo later that night to see if you needed anything, you weren't there. Imagine my surprise again when I later found out that your twin brother finally showed up for his wedding eighteen hours late?" Maggie's eyebrows disappeared behind her bangs, her eyes accusing me. "After that, it didn't take long for me to put the tiny, illicit pieces together."

Swirling the drink around in my hand, I tried not to think back on anything that had happened over the past day and a half. "And you flew down here to what? Kick my ass?"

Her leg lifted behind me, doing just that. "Now that that's done, I'm here to provide as little or as much moral support as you need. I hear that's what good friends are supposed to do for each other."

"Thanks. Friend." I managed a smile, nudging her. "So you know what happened. That at least saves me the time of explaining it."

"I don't think so, chief. Nice try though." Copying my style, Maggie leaned over the bar and snagged a beer bottle. "I might know what you did, but I don't have a damn clue *why* you did it. So make like a good book and open up already."

I shook my head as I lifted the glass to my lips. The fumes didn't make me wince anymore. Actually, there weren't even any fumes I could detect. "You know *why* I did what I did, Mags. Don't make me talk about it. I'm done talking about it. I'm done living my life with that at the center of it. I'm . . ." *What was the word again?* "Done."

"So what? The girl you've spent half your life in love with was marrying your brother and you just *had* to step in for him when he didn't show up? You know, take one for the team and do the noble, totally selfless thing?"

I wasn't looking at her, but I could hear the raised brow in her tone. "You're right. I was a selfish prick." My hand waved before I took a drink. "There. Happy now?"

"If you're a selfish prick, then Jacob is up for Cover Saint of the Year." She snorted then took a swig of her beer.

"I know why you did what you did, and it wasn't because you were looking out for yourself."

My back lowered when I exhaled. Thinking back, I couldn't exactly remember what had been going through my head when I stepped into my brother's tux. Not a lot, since time hadn't been a luxury I'd had.

"I just . . . couldn't stand to watch her heart get broken again, you know? I couldn't stand there and see her hurt by my brother one more time. I can't stand to see her in pain." My eyes closed, trying to chase the images from my mind. I'd come here to drink her away, not drink and talk about her.

"Ah, if that wasn't so pathetic, it might be the sweetest thing I've ever heard."

My teeth ground together. "Not helping."

"So you thought you'd marry her, take off on her honeymoon, and what? You'd both get the happily ever after you deserve?" Maggie's voice was soft now, her hand covering my forearm.

Maggie had gone to the same high school as all three of us and witnessed all the highs and lows of our relationships. She and I'd gone to the same med school and worked at the same hospital now, so she still got a first-row seat to the Matt in Love With the Wrong Girl Show.

"I wasn't really thinking more than five minutes into the future when I decided to pose as my brother in front of the altar."

"And I'm going to take a stab at it and say you weren't thinking more than five seconds into the future last night when you and her . . ." She took another sip of her beer.

"Maggie . . ."

"Don't lie to me. You can lie to her. Your brother. *Yourself*. But you better not even think about lying to me, because I will call you out so fast your head will spin."

Drink still in hand, I dropped my head into the web of my fingers, feeling like I could barely hold myself up anymore. What had I done? Where had things gone so wrong? What the fuck was wrong with me?

"I slept with her," I whispered. "I slept with Cora. I slept with my brother's girl."

She didn't say anything for a minute. She didn't yell or huff or shake her head at me. She just sat there quietly, like she was as out of explanations and answers as I was.

"I'm going to tell you a secret. Something I suspected a long time ago, and something I realized a few years back. I didn't tell you because I wasn't sure you had the heart to accept it, or the balls to do something about it, but after what you just admitted . . ." She blew out a low whistle and slid into the empty stool between us. She took the drink out of my hand and set it down beside her beer. Then she leaned in. "Cora's not your brother's girl." When I shook my head, she continued. "She never has been, though I know that's what he thinks and that's what she does her best to make others believe."

"What are you talking about? I'm swimming in booze over here, so I'm going to need you to spell it out for me."

She leaned in even closer, like the words she was about to speak were dangerous. "Cora's always been *your* girl. Yours." Her hand squeezed my arm tighter. "It's not Jacob she wants. It's you. It's always been you."

I'd never wanted to believe anything more in my life, but just because a person wanted to believe something, that didn't make it real. A lie could never become the truth because a person wished it so.

"She doesn't know what she wants." I picked up my drink again and drained another sip before Maggie could pull it away from me.

"Oh, she knows what she wants. She's just afraid to say it out loud."

Maggie nudged my arm, waiting for me to say something, but what was there to say? She was my good friend. She felt obligated to say what she was. She was trying to lick my wounds so when I returned the loser and my brother the victor, I'd have something to cling to. Some positive memento of Cora's and my time together—that she wanted me over my brother.

Just thinking that made me laugh.

"And if what you're saying is true, why is she so afraid to say it out loud?" I turned my head to look at her.

She blinked at me, but she looked like she wanted to smack me over the head instead. "Because our whole life, dummy, a girl's told to use her brain to get ahead in life. She's told not to be too emotional or sensitive and all of that kind of lame advice." Maggie clinked her bottle against my glass when I went to lift it to my lips. "Cora's been using her brain when it comes to her love life. Jacob was obvious about the way he felt about her. He's the one who asked her to marry him, he's the one who's been open and honest about the way he feels about her, shoddy and weak as it all is. She picked him with her brain."

My head was starting to hurt. I guessed it had more to do with what Maggie was saying than the booze.

"But it's you she knows is the right one in her gut. She knows it's you, but you haven't given her anything in return.

You're a risk, the other brother, the off-limits territory." This time when I lifted my drink, she tore the glass out of my hand and threw it over her shoulder onto the beach. "She picked you years ago, you dumb fuck, you were just too blind to see it."

Maggie's words were messing with my head, but my head was already messed up enough. I didn't need anything else adding more confusion to the mix.

"You're just saying that to make me feel better, and I appreciate it, but there's nothing you can say that will change the way Cora feels about me."

"This isn't about Cora. This is about you. This is about you being my friend and me wanting you to be happy." Maggie made a face then washed it away with the last swig of her beer.

"You never liked her," I stated, because it wasn't a question. Maggie had never been pro-Cora. Not that Cora had ever been a big fan of Maggie's either.

"It has less to do with me not liking her and more to do with me liking you. She just so happened to rip your heart out every other week, so yeah, I wasn't exactly her biggest cheerleader. Kind of hard to cozy up to the chick who makes mincemeat out of your friend's internal organs like it's her favorite pastime." Maggie waved her empty beer at the bartender, but he was still busy with the brunettes. Didn't look like his schedule would free up anytime soon either. After a minute, she just leaned over the counter and pulled another beer from the ice cooler.

"She wasn't trying to hurt me. She didn't know I liked her."

"Yeah, well, you could have been a little more forthcoming with your feelings. We women can't read minds either, you know?"

Maggie sighed when I grabbed another glass, but she didn't stop me. She must have resigned herself to the fact that I was intent on getting drunk.

"I was plenty forthcoming last night. I couldn't have been any more forthcoming," I said, thinking of how many things I'd said to her last night, how many times I'd told her I loved her with my words while my body made love to hers. "And her being up in her hotel room with my brother right now pretty much answers how she took me opening up to her."

Maggie's beer slipped away from her lips. "You're shitting me, right? She's with him right now, up there?" Twisting in her stool, her eyes ran up the length of the hotel tower looming behind us.

I kept my eyes aimed out at the ocean. It was dark, but I could still make out the stirrings of a storm. The wind was picking up, more gusty than breezy. "I wish I was shitting you."

"What a bitch," she snapped.

"Maggie."

"What?" She gave me a look, unfazed by the warning in my tone and face. "She is. If she's boning him after boning you, that's the very definition of a bitch. I never understood what you saw in her." She shook her head and stopped looking at the hotel. "You know, other than her being pretty and perky and all of those shallow things you seem way above, by the way."

I found myself almost smiling when my mind traveled back in time. Way back. Back to when I first started to realize I loved Cora Matthews. "You didn't know me until high school, so you don't know I had a speech issue growing up."

Maggie's forehead lined. "Like what? You had a lisp or something, because let me just enjoy that mental image right now."

My face flattened. "I stuttered."

"Well, shit. I'm an ass." She took the bottle from me and poured some into my glass.

"It started when I was little. I can't remember a time when I didn't stutter. When I started school, it got worse. Kids laughing, teachers telling me to just slow down and speak up, all that kind of stuff that only makes a stuttering problem worse." I shook my head, thinking about those awkward years. "Jacob stood up for me at school, so kids would usually back off eventually, but he gave it to me just as much at home when we were alone."

"Big surprise," Maggie mumbled.

"Yeah, well, he was my brother. He could kick my ass, but he'd kick anyone else's ass if they made fun of me."

"Wow. What a hero."

I lifted my glass at her and took a sip. "Dad refused to see it as a problem, so he wouldn't get me help. No son of his could have a speech impediment because, by God, he only bore strong, perfect offspring." My eyes rolled at the idiocy born of machismo. "My stuttering problem wasn't that bad, as most go, and probably could have been worked out in a year or two with a speech therapist, but since I didn't have a speech problem . . ."

Maggie and I took a drink together, filling in the blanks.

"Cora hated the way the other kids teased me. She hated the way Jacob and my dad laughed. She wanted to do something to help me, so she went to the library, checked out every book she could on stuttering, and read them all." When I realized I was smiling, I wiped at my mouth, trying to erase it. "Then she sat down with me, every single night for a solid year, and we worked together. She had me read books out loud to her. She taught me to pause and take a deep breath when I felt myself getting nervous, to recognize which words were triggers for my stuttering. She helped me, Maggie. She was the only one too." My shoulders lifted. "All it took was a year and my stuttering was pretty much gone. Shit, if it wasn't for her, I might still be that same stuttering, red-faced kid who couldn't get a sentence out without choking on it."

"You? Matt Adams? A stuttering problem?" Maggie's eyes were narrowed as she looked at me, like she couldn't believe it.

"True story."

"Good thing the shaky voice didn't translate into shaky hands, Dr. Surgeon."

She nudged me, still shaking her head like she was trying to convince herself of the story I'd just told her. "I guess Cora going into speech therapy wasn't a big surprise to you then."

"Not even the slightest."

"Well, shit." She blew out a breath. "Now you've gone and given me a reason to like the damn woman, and I was really determined to spend the rest of my life loathing her."

"Cora did a lot more for me than just that, Mags." I twisted my glass around in my hands. "That's just the tip of the iceberg."

"So you're saying you like her for more than her looks?"

"Far more than her looks. Although her looks are rather wonderful too." My phone vibrated in my pocket then, and I nearly fell off of my stool trying to get to it. The alcohol made me feel like a two-year-old trying to do papier-mâché.

When I saw the number on the display, not even close to the one I'd been hoping to find, I ground my jaw and stuffed the phone back into my pocket.

"Call girl? Mail-order bride?" Maggie tapped her fingers on the counter. "Rebounds R Us?"

"My dad." With that, I finished what was left in my glass. I needed more.

"What does he want?"

"Oh, probably just to yell, emasculate, and humiliate me. You know, before threatening to write me out of the will." I waved the bottle in the air before pouring a little more than I'd intended into my glass. If I didn't slow down, I was going to owe the bartender for the whole damn bottle.

"What? And be forced to live off your paltry surgeon's wages? That's just cruel." Maggie made an appalled face, which got a chuckle out of me.

My world was in ruins, but at least I could still see the humor in some things.

"So, Matthew Adams?" Maggie made a clicking sound with her mouth. "What are you going to do to fix this mess?"

My head tipped. "Not a damn clue." I chased that down with a nice big swig. "Sweep it under the rug? Let my brother kick my ass? Have the parts of my brain Cora's in surgically removed? Unless you have any better ideas?"

My head fell into the cradle of my hand again. I felt lost. I *was* lost. I felt like a ship on that big ocean out there, not sure where I was or what direction I needed to go. I didn't have a destination because I'd lost my compass. I was starting to wonder if I'd ever had one to being with.

Maggie must have sensed something was wrong. Well, really wrong. She scooted her stool over so it was right up against mine, and she draped her arm and half of herself over me. Her head tucked over my shoulder as she gave me a squeeze. "Listen, I know your brother has his good points." When I huffed my doubt, she added, "He's related to you."

"Maggie," I exhaled.

"And he can drink a sailor under the table." From her tone, she was amused with herself, but she cleared her throat and tried to get more serious. "You love him, I get it, and you want to do what's right, but is that worth three people living a lie their whole lives?"

CHAPTER THIRTEEN

Cora

"You mean everything to me, baby. Everything. I'm so sorry I missed the wedding. I'll never forgive myself. I'll never stop trying to make it up to you, I swear."

Jacob hadn't stopped repeating the same phrases he'd first said to me in the lobby, but I couldn't shake the feeling that with every repeat, they sounded less and less sincere. I wanted to believe him. I wanted so badly to believe him, but I couldn't ignore what had happened. I couldn't ignore the past, and I couldn't ignore the warnings going off in my head, questions as to what he'd been doing to miss what should have been one of the biggest days of our lives.

I couldn't ignore the way I felt.

I'd been doing that for years, and it had done me no favors.

As evidenced by the one person I was thinking about right now—and it wasn't the one with his arms around me, his mouth close to my ear as he repeated his promises and apologies again and again.

Matt.

Where was he?

Where had he gone?

What did he think?

Matt. Always Matt. I was so exhausted by my secret thoughts of Matt that I felt ancient inside, like my conscience had lived an eternity while my body wasn't even thirty.

"Please, let me make it up to you. Let me make this right, baby. There's nothing you and me can't get through, I know it." Jacob's mouth moved lower, tasting my throat, making me stiffen. "We're meant to be together."

The way he touched me, the way his mouth moved against me, the way his hands felt . . . why did it all feel so wrong now? For years, I'd known nothing but his touch, and now, it felt uninvited. Unwanted. It felt wrong.

All I could do was compare it to the way Matt's touch felt—how his hands had moved over me, his lips touched me, his body fit against mine.

"Jacob, stop." My voice sounded small, insignificant.

When his hands kept pressing into me, pushing me farther into the corner of the elevator until I felt like all of the oxygen had been drained from the car, I pushed him away. Harder than I'd intended. He staggered back into the opposite corner, looking at me like he didn't recognize me.

"You've been drinking. And I'm not going to have this conversation with you until you're sober."

He'd recovered and was already making his way back to me. "Who said anything about talking?"

A slow smile pulled at one side of his mouth. I remembered a time when my heart would do crazy, erratic things whenever I saw that smile aimed my way. Now, it made me sad. Sad for what had been, what could have been, and everything that had been lost.

"I've missed you, Cora. I need to feel close to you."

My fingers tightened around the handrail. "You didn't show up to our wedding. The event we'd been planning for a year, the one that five hundred people attended. I'm not okay with turning my head and forgetting it ever happened. So don't even think about it." I pushed his hand away when it went to form around my waist.

His eyes flashed, his face turning red. "Yeah, and I've already apologized for that a million times. I've promised you I'm going to spend the rest of my life making it up to you. What more do you want from me?"

When the elevator doors opened, I couldn't move fast enough. Jacob followed me, half a footstep behind, waiting for me to say something. Waiting for me to forgive him the way I had a thousand times before. It wasn't happening. Not this time. Not until he disproved my theory for why he'd missed our wedding.

"Cora, stop."

I didn't.

"Baby, please."

No way.

"Enough." With that, his arms roped around me and he pushed me up against the hall wall, fitting himself against me so I couldn't move, let alone keep walking away from him.

Jacob and I had fought like crazy over the course of ten years together, but it had never gotten physical. He'd never exerted his physical force over me like he was now, and it made me go blind with anger. Partly because he was using his strength to mold me to his will, and partly because I wasn't strong enough to fight back. Like Matt, Jacob was big and took care of his body. He was strong, fast, and he knew it.

I'd never felt more like a puppet than I did right there, shoved against some hotel wall by the man I was supposed to marry yesterday.

"Cora, I'm sorry. I just need you to stop and listen to me for a minute. I need you to slow down and hear me out." His breath was hot against my cheek and smelled of Jacob's favorite brand of scotch. I was used to the smell of it on his breath. More used to it than I was its absence. "Let me make it up to you. Let me explain. Let me. . ." His mouth was on my neck again, more frantic this time, his hands moving with the same kind of urgency.

"Jacob, enough." Without warning, I elbowed him in the stomach as hard as I could. Which wasn't all that hard since he had me pinned so tightly against the wall. Still, it sent him back a few steps so I could turn around and back away.

One hand was covering his stomach where I'd just elbowed him, his light eyes so dark they couldn't have possibly still been blue. "This is about him, isn't it? You let that fucker touch you and make you feel good, and now you can't stand a real man's touch anymore?"

My mouth fell open. "Jacob—"

"You got your wish, didn't you? You finally got a chance to see what my brother was like in bed. Was it good? Could he make you feel better than me? Did you like the feel of his cock in your mouth better than mine?"

"That is enough!" I hadn't meant to shout—we'd probably already gotten all of this floor's attention already—but I couldn't help it. "How dare you turn this around on me! You were the one who started this whole sequence of events. Matt was the one who stepped in to try to help, and here you are, accusing me like I planned all of this."

Jacob's chest was rising and falling quickly, his shirt twisted and his eyes wild. "So you did fuck him?"

My eyes narrowed. That was all he cared about. If I did or didn't sleep with his twin brother. "I'm not having this conversation with you when you've been drinking. So sober up and come find me. Then we can talk."

I'd been planning to head back to my room to change since Jacob had suggested going on a walk to talk, but now that that talk wasn't going to happen, I wasn't going anywhere close to my room. Not with Jacob looking at me the way he was now—like he couldn't decide if he'd rather hit me or screw me.

"Where are you going?" His voice was quieter, the notes of anger gone.

"Out." I was halfway back to the elevators.

Punching the down button, I kept checking down the hall to make sure he wasn't coming after me. He wasn't. He was frozen to the wall where he'd staggered back, his head hanging and his expression blank.

His head lifted, his eyes finding mine. "I love you."

I glanced away. I knew from experience I caved whenever he became the brooding, self-loathing version he was evolving into now. "Then start showing it."

The elevator doors opened right then, and I lunged inside, punching the first floor button. After the doors closed, I undid my heels and took them off. I was still planning on going for a walk—alone. I needed to figure out what was going on. Inside my head. Inside my heart. I needed to, once and for all, confront the feelings I had for them both and decide who I belonged with, if either of them.

If either of them even wanted me when all was said and done, because I couldn't be with Jacob without telling him about Matt. And I couldn't be with Matt without confronting the reality that I'd been with his brother for years.

When the doors opened on the first floor, I slipped out and left through one of the side hotel doors that put me closest to the beach. Sand between my toes, ocean waves crashing beside me—it sounded like the perfect way to work out years of repressed feelings.

I loved Jacob. I knew that. But I wasn't sure it was the kind of love that one should have for the person they planned to spend their whole life with. I loved the person he was when he wasn't drinking, and I had come to fear who he was when he had been.

It was quiet everywhere tonight; that probably had to do with the storm coming. Or possibly coming, because no one seemed to know for sure if it would hit us or not. The lack of a crowd made for that much better of a walk. I needed time alone with my thoughts to attempt to untangle the web I'd spun in the years since I'd met the Adams brothers. I was no longer sure who I felt what for, that's how interwoven they'd become.

Only a few steps onto the beach, I recognized a familiar laugh. Instantly, I felt my smile forming and all of the heaviness inside me start to lift.

Matt. He was close by. Maybe I could talk this whole mess out with him and he could provide some clarity. For years I'd gone to him when I needed someone to talk to, although this might not be the ideal topic to discuss with him since it had to do with him. And my feelings for him.

My feet moved faster. I could no longer hear his laughter, but I felt his presence. Up ahead, the hotel's beach bar was glowing, but unlike earlier today, it was mostly empty. A handful of people were scattered around at the stools, but all I saw was him. It was kind of amusing to see Matt pressed up against the counter of some cheesy beach bar—so not his scene—but that was when I noticed he wasn't alone.

Not alone at all.

There was a woman on the stool next to him, but really, she was as close to him as she could get before she was on his lap. My feet stopped moving as an ache spread from my chest. Her hands were all over him, and he was doing nothing to push her away. Her head was close to his, and the two of them looked at each other in a way . . . that I was not going to let myself think about.

Between them on the counter was a half-empty bottle of something, and after Matt poured some of it into his glass, he slid it in front of her. She drained it in one drink, her eyebrow lifting at him right after.

I didn't see what happened next. I couldn't stay to watch. Instead, I turned and ran in the opposite direction, as quickly as I could in the soft sand while wearing a dress not designed for jogging.

It wasn't until I tasted the saltiness on my lips that I realized I'd started crying. Over what I'd seen, over what was about to happen, over this whole damn mess.

I shouldn't even be so upset that I'd just caught him with some other woman—I had no claim to him. We were friends. He'd done what he had at the wedding because of that. He'd done what we had that night because we'd both been tipsy, I'd been all over him, and he was a red-blooded man. I might have thought he was Jacob . . . but now I wasn't even so sure of that.

Did I really believe last night that he was Jacob? Or did I know the truth inside me?

Even that I couldn't make sense of anymore.

Facing the fact that I felt like I didn't know a goddamned thing anymore brought on a fresh flood of tears that dropped me to the sand. I was tired of running. Tired of burying my feelings.

I wasn't taking another step until I confronted the harshest reality of all—was I in love with Jacob or his brother?

CHAPTER FOURTEEN

Matt

The next morning was painful. I had a whole new respect for the hangover and how clear liquid could make a person feel like their brain was about to start liquefying out their ears.

I awoke with a groan, reaching for the bottle of aspirin I kept on my nightstand. Except it wasn't there . . . because I wasn't in my condo in Miami. I was on St. Thomas. On my brother's and Cora's honeymoon.

My head pulsed harder with that reminder.

Cora.

How could one woman invoke so much pain, and at the same time so much joy, when I thought about her? It didn't seem possible, but I knew better. I had countless years of evidence proving it.

"What in the hell were you thinking?"

The voice was guarded and controlled, coming from the side of the room. I'd known it wouldn't take long for my brother to confront me, but it could have come at a better time. Like when I didn't feel like each verbalized word was sticking another pin in the cushion that was my corneal matter.

Forcing my eyes to open, I found him leaning into the wall across from me, arms crossed, dark hollows beneath his eyes.

"I was thinking about Cora."

His chest puffed out when he exhaled. "You were thinking about yourself."

"Fuck off." I wasn't in the mood for my brother's accusations, not since he was the first domino that sent the whole carefully constructed maze tumbling down.

"Speaking of fucking . . ." Jacob shoved off the wall, moving a few steps toward the bed. I didn't miss the way he inspected it, like he was half expecting to find Cora naked and sprawled out beside me. "Did you?" He sniffed. "With Cora?"

"And good morning to you too, brother. Nice to see you." I rolled over onto my back and attempted to sit up. I hated vodka. I was never coming within arm's reach of it again. Ever. "I make it a habit not to have long, drawn-out conversations with a hangover, so you're just going to have to ask Cora if you need an answer to that right this second."

I tried to keep my affect flat, giving nothing away. Why was he asking me? Shouldn't he know either way, whatever she'd decided to tell him, by now? I couldn't imagine it wasn't the first thing he'd wanted to know last night when he confronted her.

"I tried asking her. She wouldn't say a damn thing about it."

When Jacob moved closer, I could see he was still in the same clothes from last night. They weren't as fresh and pressed-looking as they'd been, and I didn't want to think why that was. I didn't want to consider why it looked like he'd gotten no sleep either. There was only so much a man could take, and my limit had been reached last night when I'd watched her run into his arms again, for the millionth damn time, when my arms were just as open and willing.

"Too busy making up?" My voice took on a sharp edge as I sat up a little higher, propping the pillow behind me.

"Maybe," Jacob answered instantly, but then he turned to look out the window. Thank god it was overcast, because sunlight would not be my friend at the moment.

"*Maybe* you made up?" I asked, unable to help it. There were two ways a couple could make up, and I knew there was only one way where Jacob was concerned. I needed to know what, if anything, had been said last night before . . . the other making up happened.

"Barely," he admitted, his arms bracing against the wall as he stared out the window absently. I wasn't used to seeing Jacob like this—lost, unsure. That was more the look I carried around. "She barely let me touch her, couldn't stand to have me close. Which is a first." His head turned, accusation darkening his eyes. "So something's up. You said something. Or you did something." He was quiet a moment, like he was giving me a chance to speak up, but it didn't last long. "I know you've had a thing for her forever. Finally made your move—by pretending to be me. Genius plan there, Matt. But you're the brains in the family, right?"

Forcing myself to take a breath, my hands curling into the sheets. "Let me remind you, MIA Groom, that the whole reason I did what I did was to save your ass."

"More like you were trying to get the piece of ass you've been wanting since puberty."

My jaw ground together. "That's Cora you're talking about. Watch it."

Jacob pushed off the wall, turning from the window. "Yeah, and she's mine to defend. Not yours."

"Thanks for the brotherly reminder." My hand ran through my hair. It felt like half of it was plastered to my head from how I'd been sleeping.

Something on my hand caught Jacob's eye. "That's my ring. I want it." His eyes narrowed further the longer he looked at it on my finger.

"And you can have it once you tell Cora what you were doing that kept you detained from your wedding." My left hand curled into a fist. The ring had only been there a couple of days, and already it felt like it belonged there. Even though I knew it wasn't mine.

Jacob's face changed color, but he stayed where he was. I'd expected him to charge me, to try to rip the damn ring from my finger when I didn't willingly give it back, but he wasn't moving. Which was lucky for me, since I wasn't in the best condition to hold my own against my brother—not that he looked much better.

"I want it, Matt."

"And I will happily hand it over once you explain to her why you missed your own damn wedding, Jacob."

His arms folded over his chest as he paced. He was still managing to hold back, which had never been a characteristic my brother was known for. "I need to know. I need to know if you slept with her. No more of this 'ask her' bullshit. You're my brother. You look me in the eye and tell me either way."

Well at least he'd moved on from the wedding ring—not that this subject was any less dangerous.

"And she needs to know what you were doing that night before and the day of the wedding." I reached for a glass of water on the nightstand, guessing Maggie was responsible for it. I didn't remember much from last night—half a bottle of vodka would do that to a person—but she must have gotten my drunk ass back here somehow and left a glass of water for me for when I eventually woke up and realized I wanted to die.

Jacob was pacing, looking like a wild animal who'd just been caged. This was when he was most dangerous—when he felt trapped, cornered, and didn't have the upper hand.

Instead of backing off as I had before, I kept pressing on. "Tell her. You be honest with her, and she'll be honest with you."

His head shook. "I was hungover off my ass that next morning. You remember. We were drinking like crazy that night, my last one as a bachelor. I was lucky I woke up at all with all the booze you let me down." He didn't look at me; he just kept pacing. He didn't look at me because he knew better—I wasn't the person to blame for his excessive drinking.

"Don't lie to me. Don't lie to her. I know, Jacob. I know." I finished the whole cup of water, hoping it might dull the anger coursing through me. It only seemed to make it worse.

"You know jack shit."

"You know jack shit if you chose that girl from the bar, any girl from any fucking place in the world, over the one you already had." My hands were squeezing the glass so hard, I was surprised it didn't break. "You know jack shit, because you had it all. You had everything, and you threw it all away for nothing."

He stopped moving, his head turning toward me. "I *still* have everything. I *still* have her. I didn't lose anything. I didn't throw away anything. Cora still belongs to me." He drove his fist into his chest, the vein running down his forehead bursting through his skin.

"I didn't realize she was something to own." My voice was a stark contrast to his—tamed where his was wild. "Who were you with that night?"

"None of your damn business."

My brow lifted at him. "Maybe not, but it is hers."

Jacob picked up his pacing. He was acting erratic, unsure, not at all how I was used to seeing my brother. This whole thing had undone him as much as it had me. Turned him into someone else.

"You better not tell her. You better not say a fucking word."

"Then you'd better tell her. Soon." My gaze wandered out the window now that my eyes had semi-adjusted. The sky was every shade of gray in the spectrum, the ocean so dark it looked black. The palm leaves were shuddering in the wind, and I couldn't see a single soul on the beach. The storm didn't seem to be moving in another direction or dissolving. "Where is she?"

"Who?"

I exhaled, guessing that was a question my brother needed clarified. "Cora. Where is she?"

"I don't know. She wouldn't answer her phone. Wasn't in her hotel room when I stopped by earlier."

I was in the middle of coaxing my body out of bed when I froze. "*Her* hotel room? As in, you had a different one?"

Jacob snorted, tying his hands behind his neck as he continued pacing. "Yeah, not exactly what I had in mind, but I had to sleep somewhere. Her room door was as sealed shut as her legs last night."

At the same time I wanted to punch him for talking about her like that, I kind of wanted to kiss him too. They hadn't slept together—they hadn't even slept in the same room. All because of her. Why hadn't she let Jacob in? Why hadn't she let him close like she had so many times before when he'd messed up and apologized?

I was a damn fool to think it had anything to do with me, but what other explanation was there? Why else would she not let the man she'd promised to marry into her room last night? Yeah, she had a reason to be seriously pissed about the wedding fiasco, but was there more?

Was I the more?

The only way to know for sure was to find her.

Sliding out of bed, I pushed through the hangover and jogged into the bathroom to crank on the shower. I smelled terrible and figured Cora had enough experience with Jacob showing up smelling like death warmed over from a night of drinking—she didn't need me showing up the same way.

"There's a storm coming, and instead of looking for Cora, you're here getting in my face?" I asked.

I pulled a bottle of water out of the mini fridge just outside the bathroom and tossed it at Jacob. He needed to sober up and, from the looks of him, take a shower too. No matter what went down today, we were all going to be truthful with each other. Once and for all. No more lies. No more deceit. The truth.

I wasn't sure if that would mean I'd lose her and my brother in the same day, but was keeping them close with lies so much better?

"Hey, for the record?" Jacob's voice was muffled by the sound of the shower as I crawled inside. "I don't think you did it. I don't believe you could do that kind of thing to me . . . but I just need to hear one of you say it. You know?"

We were both quiet long enough for me to drop my head in the shower and feel like a total piece of shit for sleeping with the woman he claimed to love. Jacob might have done some nasty things to me, but he'd never gone so far as to sleep with the girl I was with. Not that he'd had many opportunities to do so.

"I know the feeling," I whispered, letting the hot water beat down my back as I tried to figure out what was right and what was wrong.

I wondered if there was any such thing as right anymore. I knew it was wrong for me to love Cora, but just the same, it was the most right thing I'd ever felt.

When I hopped out of the shower a couple minutes later, Jacob was gone. I wasn't sure if he'd gone back to his hotel room or out to search for Cora or more in search of a drink, but he was gone.

After throwing on the first clothes my fingers came across in my suitcase, I slid into a pair of sandals and flew out the door. Despite the wind, it wasn't cold, much like the storms we got in Miami. The wind was strong, but nothing compared to some of the storms I remembered from back home. It wasn't as bad as I thought it would be.

Jogging toward the hotel, figuring I'd start searching there, I pulled out my phone and tried calling her. The call went immediately to voicemail, so either her phone was dead or turned off. I tried once more before punching in another number.

"It's barely nine in the morning and you chugged about a pint of shitty vodka last night. What are you doing up right now?" Maggie yawned, but I knew she hadn't been asleep. She'd always been an early riser, plus med school had gotten us accustomed to long nights and minimal sleep.

"Mind recapping last night for me? Just so I know who I have to apologize to?"

"Besides me for having to wrangle your drunk ass all the way back to that loveshack cabin on the opposite end of the hotel grounds that you thought was such a great idea?" Maggie snorted. "You need to go on a diet, because I felt like I was wrestling an elephant last night."

As soon as I lunged into the lobby, I scanned every chair and corner in the place. Other than the employees and an older couple snoring with papers spread open in their laps, no one else was there. "Have you seen her?"

"Who?"

I continued to scan the lobby, cradling the phone on my shoulder. "Cora? Have you seen Cora?"

"I'm in a hotel on the other side of the island because that's how much space I need from you people. What makes you think I've seen her?" There was a brief pause. "Wait? Does that mean she's missing or something?"

Sticking my head into the couple of restaurants and the lounge ended in the same result—no Cora. "Jacob hasn't seen her since last night. She's not answering her phone."

Instead of going to the elevators and trying her room, I went back outside. Cora wasn't in her room—if she wanted to be alone, she wouldn't be hiding in the most obvious place people would look for her.

"Wait. Hold up. So there was a runaway groom and now a runaway wife?" Maggie let out a whistle. "God, I can't get this much drama even with my cable subscription."

As I made my way along some of the walking paths winding around the resort, the ball in my throat grew. Where was she? "You haven't seen her? Promise?"

"No," Maggie answered immediately.

"Would you tell me if you had?"

She laughed like my question was amusing. "Yes, believe it or not, I would. You turned me Team Cora with your final story last night of why you fell head over heels for her." She paused like she was waiting for me to catch up, but I didn't have a damn clue what I'd said last night. With the way I was feeling and the amount of alcohol I'd consumed, I could have said just about anything. "You know, when your date to freshmen homecoming stood you up and Miss Cora went with you instead since your asshole brother was getting asshole drunk and passed out? So she went with you and you pretended to be Jacob and no one was the wiser—Jacob especially, since he spent the night in a drunken stupor in your dad's pool house."

My feet stopped rushing along the pavement. "I told you about that?" I sighed, reminding myself why excessive drinking was to be avoided at all costs. If not for my liver's sake, my dignity's. "That was a secret both of us were supposed to take to the grave."

Maggie made a clucking sound with her tongue. "Well, when Jacob finds out about what happened between you two here, the grave's not too far off for you, I'm guessing."

"Funny." I started moving again, and when I reached the end of the hotel grounds, I journeyed onto the beach. No one was lounging on the sand today. Even the beach bar from hell was boarded shut. "If you hear anything, will you let me know?"

"Like you even need to ask. And if things start getting really juicy, right before you're all about to sit down and have that heart-to-heart, let me know so I can be there in full-body Kevlar. I wouldn't want to miss it."

Ignoring her request, I jogged down the beach. "How long are you here for?"

I couldn't remember if I'd asked her how long she was staying, where she was staying, or when her flight was heading out. All I remembered was that she'd shown up for moral support after hearing through the grapevine about her friend, Matt Adams, posing as Jacob Adams at the wedding the Miami muckety-mucks would be talking about for months.

"I'm staying as long as you need me," she said, pausing. "Which hopefully isn't any longer than three days because I promised work I'd be back by then. They're a little short-staffed since someone decided to go and take a week vacation for his brother's wedding."

I'd taken the week figuring I'd need some "alone time" after watching Cora marry Jacob, not because I'd be playing stand-in groom. It was almost like I'd planned it. Or some higher power had. "What did I do to deserve such a good friend?"

Maggie snorted. "You're Matt Adams, you dummy. Everybody likes you. It's a universal law of the planet or something. Stop acting so surprised that people dig you so much." She made a clucking sound with her mouth. "Or that a certain someone might just happen to love you."

That was a dangerous topic. Dangerous for what it meant for Jacob, Cora, and me.

"I'll check in later with an update. Thanks again for flying in and wrangling my fat elephant ass back to the cabin last night."

"Yeah, well, I might have groped it as a means of payment, so we're square."

After saying good-bye, I stuffed the phone back into my pocket and continued searching. She wasn't on the beach. She wasn't anywhere in or close to the hotel. Shit, this was a big island. She could have gone just about anywhere.

Just as I was about to head back toward the lobby to call for a cab, I thought of one more place to look. The same place she'd gone yesterday morning after waking up and discovering who she'd really exchanged 'I dos' with.

The trees and bushes provided a little break from the wind, and it didn't take me long to remember the path I'd taken yesterday. I found her in the exact same spot, sitting there and staring at the ocean like she had before.

She was in the same blue dress from last night, her hair tied back in a loose braid and her makeup almost totally washed away. She'd been crying. From the dark trails streaking down her cheeks, she'd cried a lot.

My chest ached from seeing her like this, knowing she'd been sad and alone. Knowing she'd been crying and had no one close by to comfort her.

When I continued closer, coming around the side so she could see me, she didn't flinch.

"There's a storm coming." I stuffed my hands in my pockets to keep from reaching out to her. I had no idea what had happened last night or how she felt this morning. I knew that last night I'd felt betrayed that she'd run to Jacob, forgetting all about me, but after my brother's and my talk this morning, I wasn't so sure if that's the way things really were.

"No shit." A single-noted laugh came from her. "I just slept with my fiancé's brother, who I might or might not be legally married to. The storm's already swept us up, Matt."

My teeth bit into the inside of my cheek. "I wasn't trying to trick you when I put that ring on your finger."

"Then what were you trying to do?"

That was the same question I'd been asking myself, and I'd come up with a dozen different answers. "I was trying to help you." I shifted, rubbing at the back of my head. "I figured Jacob would probably show up shit-faced or something eventually and no one but him and I would have to know what had happened. I wanted to save you the embarrassment of him not standing at your side in front of a crowd of people. Like he used to."

"Like he used to?" she repeated, curling her feet beneath her. "What does that mean?"

I gave her a moment to take her question back. A moment to move on to something else. When she finally turned her head to look at me, waiting for an answer, I sighed. "During the two years of high school you two were together, he never once walked with you to a class, or sat with you at lunch, or so much as glanced your way while at school."

Her throat moved when she swallowed. "How could he? We were trying to keep it a secret from your dad."

"He was trying to keep you a secret from more than just our dad, Cora," I whispered, ashamed for saying it but unable to help myself. She wasn't blind. She had to know why.

"You're an ass." She glared at me before looking back out at the dark, surging ocean.

"You asked for the truth from me from now on. You didn't ask for me to be the good guy continuing to feed you lies to protect you. So which way do you want it? Because you can't have it both ways."

She was quiet for a minute. "Okay, so you stepped in to help Jacob and me at the wedding. I could maybe wrap my head around that if I tried really, really hard. But why in the hell did you crawl into bed with me that night? Why did you —"

"Because I'm weak," I said, shifting again. I couldn't get comfortable.

"Please, Matt, you've always been strong. One of the strongest people I've ever known."

Was I? Did she really think that? "I'm weak where you're concerned. I always have been. And that night, when you put your hands on me, I couldn't do the right thing like I knew I should have. When I saw what you wanted from me in your eyes, I had to give it to you."

Her arms curled around herself, a sharp exhale spilling past her lips. "You gave it to me all right. Four separate times. Almost five."

Almost five. "Yeah, except that fifth time, you knew who I was."

I chanced a step closer. It only made her scoot away, maintaining the distance between us. I hated watching her slide away from me—I hated myself giving her a reason to do it.

"You knew exactly who I was when you were saying my name and pushing yourself against me. So now who are you going to blame for that?"

"Shut up." Her voice was small, almost silent.

"No, I won't. I've kept my mouth shut with you too many times. No more. You're going to hear the truth, and it's me who's going to tell it to you."

"Shut. Up." Her voice was louder, her expression lethal, but I didn't back down.

"You picked the wrong guy to marry."

The look she gave me right then—I'd never forget it. I guessed I'd carry it with me in my next life too, it was that loathsome. "I did not."

My arm came out at my side. "He didn't show up to his own fucking wedding. How can you expect him to show up for anything else in life?"

She twisted toward me, glaring up at me like she'd never hated anything more than she did me right then. "Well I guess I'll never get a chance to know, right? Because I think when I mention the whole 'letting his brother go down on me after he'd screwed me' thing, our relationship isn't going to go so well."

Her words hit me like a punch to the gut. They struck me silent. They must have had the same effect on her because both of us stayed like that for a while, not moving, barely seeming to breathe.

She was angry at me, or she hated me, or both. Why? Because of what I'd said just now? Because of what I'd done before? For some other reason I had yet to determine?

I'd done plenty of stupid things in my life that Cora had been a victim to, but she'd never acted so hurt before. All I could think of was how the ones we loved the most were capable of hurting us the most.

"I haven't taken it off yet." Her voice was a stark contrast to how it had sounded the last time she spoke.

I didn't understand what she was talking about until I glanced at her lap, where she was staring at the ring on her left hand.

"I haven't taken mine off either."

"Why haven't I?" Her head turned toward me. "Why haven't you?"

"I don't know."

"Yeah, I know you don't." She exhaled, smiling sadly at the ocean. "You never know, do you? With me, you're never sure."

My brows came together. "What does that mean?"

"It means one minute you're saying things, doing things, that make me think you might have feelings for me. You might have *more* than just feelings for me, and the next, you're at a bar with a strange woman who you stumble back to your room with. Into the same exact bed you fucked me in the night before." She circled the ring on her finger absently, looking like she was talking to herself instead of me. "What am I supposed to take from that? How am I supposed to make sense of it?"

My mind went blank.

"Just . . . never mind. You have a right to do whatever you want to whoever you want. It's not like you're my boyfriend." She started to stand, looking like she wanted to get out of here and away from me.

But I couldn't let her go. Not now. Maybe not ever.

My brain finally caught up to what she must have been talking about. "Last night? Are you talking about the woman I was with last night?"

She was crouching on the ground, not getting up but not sitting back down. "Sorry, I suppose I should have clarified that. I'm sure it gets confusing trying to keep all of the women in your life straight. But yes, specifically, the one you were with last night."

Another mind blank. Was she talking about me? Or someone else? "All of the women in my life? As in you and my friend Maggie, who you saw me with last night?"

Her eyes went wide like she was realizing something. "That was Maggie?"

"Yes, of course that was Maggie."

"What's she doing here?" she asked.

"She found out what happened. Wanted to provide moral support or be present to identify a body."

Cora shook her head, but I didn't miss how different she looked now compared to when I first showed up. More peaceful somehow, relieved. "So you two didn't . . ."

She didn't finish her sentence. She didn't have to. Her anger at me just now was making sense. It was almost like she was . . . *jealous?*

"No. Absolutely not. She's my friend. We're friends, nothing more." I crouched beside her, gauging her reaction at having me close. She didn't flinch or scoot away; she almost seemed to welcome it. "Now that I've explained that, you need to explain why you seem to believe I have so many women in my life."

She sat, turning slightly so she was angled toward me. The way the wind was playing with the hem of her dress was distracting me. Badly.

"Just what Jacob's mentioned. It's not like I know who they are or anything, but clearly plenty of women know you."

I had to look away from her fluttering hem and the skin it was exposing.

"It's okay. You don't have to confirm or deny it. I know you're not the type who kisses and tells."

"Jacob said this, right? Told you about all of these 'women'?" I asked.

She nodded.

"And my ladies' man reputation has been going on for how long now?" I sure as hell wasn't aware of it.

Cora was looking at me like I was playing a game with her. "Since high school."

High school. The same time she and Jacob got together. The same time my womanizing ways started. Not exactly a coincidence.

"Sophomore year?" I said.

"I don't remember exactly." She picked up a leaf that had blown into her lap and turned it over like she was searching for something. "But yeah, it was right before Thanksgiving break our sophomore year." When she looked up to see the look on my face, she added, "Give or take."

My back went rigid as I put the pieces together. The same time she and Jacob got together, he started telling her I was pretty much a manwhore. Which I was nothing even remotely close to. If that title belonged to anyone, it was my brother. Why? Why had he gone so out of his way to try to convince Cora that I was so worthless in the relationship department?

She'd mentioned he'd accused her of harboring feelings for me. What if she really had? What if she still did?

The answer should have been obvious. It should have been so clear it was blinding. I had all of the evidence to support it; why hadn't I seen it before? I was an Ivy League-educated doctor who'd come out the top of my class—in all of them. And I was the biggest idiot to have ever walked the earth.

"There aren't any other women, Cora." My hand reached for hers still turning over the leaf. "There never have been any other women."

Wasn't it obvious? Hadn't it always been? There'd only ever been you.

"Really?" Her fingers wove through mine, turning over in my hand.

I covered her hand with my other hand. "Really."

A smile started to form on her face. "I didn't really think so. You didn't seem like the type."

"Then what type do you think I am?"

Her fingers brushed across the band on my finger. "The committed type."

My smile matched hers, careful and unsure. She had no idea just how committed I was. How devoted I'd been to her when she'd never been mine to begin with.

"I need to tell you something." I lowered my head so it was aligned with hers. "I've needed to tell you something for a long time, and I know this might not seem like the right time with everything going on, but this might be the only time I'm stupid enough to say it."

The breath she'd been taking cut short. "This might be the only time I'm stupid enough to tell you something too."

A gust of wind powered over us, but I didn't think either of us really even noticed it.

"Ladies first?"

Her head whipped side to side, her smile still holding. "Definitely not in this case."

I'd been waiting for this moment for what felt like my whole life, never thinking it would actually happen, but here I was, about to say it out loud. I wasn't even nervous. Probably because it was the most real thing I'd ever known.

Something over my shoulder caught her eye, and her face changed instantly. I knew who it was before she said a thing.

"Oh look, you found her." Jacob finished climbing the trail and stood in front of us. His eyes latched on to where my hands were still covering hers. "I'm sure you were just about to call and let me know." He forced a smile, but it didn't disguise the anger I saw burning in his eyes.

When Jacob's eyes stayed locked on our hands, Cora slid hers out from mine and folded it into her lap. She put on a convincing face, like we were innocent of whatever Jacob was silently accusing us of being guilty of.

"Cora, can we talk now?" He moved closer, holding his hand out for her. "I'm sobered up—planning on staying that way. I'm ready. If you are."

She didn't take his hand. She stayed seated across from me. "Um, I don't know. Matt and I were talking."

Her eyes met mine again like she was waiting for me to say or do something. I wasn't sure what. Did she want me to blurt out what I'd been about to tell her before Jacob showed up? Did she want me to throw her over my shoulder and run away? Did she want me to throw myself into the ocean and make it easier on all three of us?

"I'm sure whatever Matt has to say to you can wait." Jacob lifted his chin at me, but he couldn't look at me. "Can't it, brother?"

It had only been waiting years to be said. "Yeah. It can."

I cleared my throat as I rose to my feet, not realizing I'd held out my hand to help her up until she'd taken it. Beside us, Jacob's jaw twitched, his hand falling back at his side.

Cora hadn't intentionally taken my hand over his—I could tell by the flash of regret on her face. It had come from a place of instinct. When she had a choice between whose hand to grab, she'd chosen mine.

"So we'll talk later?" she asked me as they started down the trail.

Jacob interjected. "If you two have anything to talk about after we're done working things out, baby." His comment was as much a threat for me as it was a promise to her.

I watched her walk away with him, but this time, she was watching me as she left. "We will."

CHAPTER FIFTEEN

Cora

He'd been about to say it. Or something close to it. I knew it.

Or at least I *thought* I knew it.

The way he'd been looking at me, the way he'd been fighting with his words, I thought Matt had been about to tell me something I'd waited years to hear from him. I mean, sure, he'd said them to me that first night on the island, but he'd been playing Jacob at the time, and I knew that had been the only reason he'd said them. He'd been saying them as Jacob, not as Matt.

Little did Matt know Jacob had never said those three words to me with half as much meaning as Matt had while faking them and pretending to be someone else.

Of course that would be the time Jacob would show up and essentially ruin the moment. He'd done that a lot, especially early on, when I'd first moved into the house with my mom. Whenever Matt and I would go play foosball together, or whenever we'd decide to watch a movie, or whatever the two of us had tried to do alone, Jacob always seemed to intervene.

I hadn't thought much of it as a kid, assuming that as twins, the two of them were inseparable and where one was, the other wanted to be. It wasn't that though. It was because Jacob had thought from the very beginning that he had some claim to me, just as I was finally starting to realize he still thought he did. Although the claim had matured into ownership.

He was the one who'd asked me to marry him, and I was the one who'd agreed. But that didn't equate to ownership. At least, I hoped that wasn't how marriage worked. It wasn't like I'd had many shining examples of marriage in my own life.

I didn't want to be owned. I didn't want to be someone's possession they could take off the shelf and put back whenever they wanted.

It was odd how one day could change a person's whole perspective on their life; I felt like I'd just awoken from some dream I'd been living for years.

"Please, baby, don't run off like that again. I was worried about you." Jacob was still leading the way down the trail I'd taken to get out here, but I could tell he was waiting for me to take his hand as I had hundreds of times before.

Not this time.

It was exhausting to be the only one who reached for the other when it didn't have to do with sex. Taxing to be the one who gave and gave until they felt run dry.

"I needed to think," was all I said.

"About what?" When Jacob glanced back at my face, he sighed. "Never mind. Dumb question."

He kept moving, checking over his shoulder every few steps to make sure I was there. It was like he was afraid I was going to run away or disappear again. I wasn't used to Jacob being so attentive and, well, acting like he gave a shit.

"Did you have enough time to get everything worked out?" he asked as the trail opened up to the beach.

My eyes stayed forward, his locked on me. "No. It's difficult to work things out when I don't have your side of the story as to what happened the day of the wedding."

Jacob's jaw moved, like it had locked up and he had to work it loose. "Well, that's what I thought we'd spend today getting out in the open. The wedding day." He sniffed, his eyes flashing. "The wedding *night*." He rolled his neck a few times. "And everything after. We've both got some explaining to do."

I nodded as we headed down the beach, keeping a step behind him. The wind was stronger out here, the storm clouds more daunting. I couldn't understand why no one besides us was on the beach though. It was beautiful. Everyone came to the beach for the blue sky and calm water, but the scene right now was just as, if not more, beautiful. A person just had to look a little closer to find the beauty in the midst of the storm.

"I booked the two of us a day at the hotel's spa. I thought it would be the perfect way to talk and figure things out between us." Jacob checked his watch. "I found you just in time. I made our appointment for ten."

I wanted to remind him that he hadn't found me—Matt had. But I knew that wouldn't be helpful to any of us.

"No, not the spa." My voice sounded strong, which made me feel even stronger.

Jacob's head turned toward me. "You love the spa. It's the perfect kind of day to spend at the spa."

"No, *you* love the spa. And I loved you and part of that was going and doing the things you loved." I couldn't believe I had finally said that. Words I'd practiced in my head but had never had the courage to bring to life.

"What do you mean? Of course you love the spa. We go all the time."

From the look on his face, he was truly surprised. He hadn't had a clue, and that shouldn't have come as a surprise. Jacob had always been so focused on himself and his wants, there wasn't much left over to notice anyone else's wants.

"No, I don't like having strangers touch me. I don't like the music or the smells or walking around in big bathrobes all day with other people." I started to walk faster, getting ahead of him as the hotel came into view. "I'm not having this conversation with you at a spa. Thank you for trying, but no, I'm not in the mood to get into an argument in front of a bunch of strange people in what's supposed to be a serene place."

"Who says we're going to get in an argument?" Jacob almost had to jog to keep up with my pace.

"Experience. The topic. The possible explanations." My eyebrow lifted at him. "Take your pick."

"Fine, I'll cancel the spa." He pulled out his phone. "Did you have something else in mind?" His tipped smile settled into place as his eyes ran down me.

My dress was a rumpled, dirty mess, and I felt like the rest of me kept with that theme. Jacob was looking at me like there wasn't a flaw on me though. Not a single one. That was one of the things he'd always done well—made me feel special when he looked at me like that. It might have only been for a moment, and they might have come few and far between, but for however long it was, I knew I meant something to him.

"Maybe one of our rooms?" he suggested.

"Jacob, please don't make me regret my decision to leave with you."

"Regret your decision to leave Matt for me?" His voice wobbled once.

"Regret my decision to leave with you to have this discussion."

My response didn't seem to appease him, but his jealousy where Matt was concerned ran deep. He could catch me merely making eye contact with his twin brother and go off. I didn't want to think about what would happen when I told him what had happened between us. Way, way more than making eye contact.

"Shit, Cora. I'm an asshole." He rubbed his forehead as we wound up the path toward the hotel. "I'm sorry about last night—I'm sorry about suggesting that again right now. I should have realized you'd need some space and not been so forceful. I was just so relieved to see you. So desperate to be close to you."

"There are more ways to be close to a person than sex."

A few heads turned as we came in the lobby, probably because I looked like I'd just played a game of tag with the storm. Jacob ground his jaw when he noticed, then he slid out of his jacket and tucked it over my shoulders. He quickly led me back toward the elevators, his hands just barely curved around my shoulders.

"What did you have in mind? I'm game for anything. Just please, give me a chance to work this out?" He spun me around before touching the up button, waiting.

"I want to go on a hike. There's a good one farther inland that passes by an old sugar plantation. I was planning on doing it when we came down here, and here we are." I shrugged, waiting.

"A hike? In this weather?" Jacob blinked.

"The weather isn't that bad. Some rain and wind. I've hiked in worse."

"A hike?" Jacob repeated, like it wasn't computing.

"I like to hike."

"Since when?"

I shifted. Jacob had never accompanied me on any of the hikes I'd gone on. I'd asked plenty of times at first, but had gotten to a point where I didn't ask anymore because I already knew his answer. "Since I was thirteen and went on my first hike in the Everglades."

"And you went on this first hike that started your life-long love affair with the hobby with whom?"

He knew. From the darkness bleeding into his eyes, I knew he knew.

"Matt took me," I said, trying to keep all emotion out of my voice. God knew it wasn't easy, not with everything happening between Matt and me. Not with everything I thought he had been about to say to me out there.

"Of course he did." Jacob bit back whatever he was going to say right after that. Instead, he took a few slow breaths then hit the up button again. "Why don't you go get changed for this hike? I'll wait here and see if I can find a cab to drive us."

When the elevator door chimed open behind me, I barely noticed. Had Jacob just gone along with my hike suggestion? Without so much as a few rounds of debate? Had he just suggested he wait here so I could have my space instead of being an opportunist and coming to my room with me? Hoping for a little time delay between wardrobe changes?

When he lifted his brows, waving toward the open doors, I guessed I had my answer.

"I'll be right here," he said, backing up to lean into the wall.

When the doors closed behind me, a million things fired in my mind. Some about Jacob. Some about Matt. Some even about me and deciding what I felt for these two men in my life. Who did I think I loved? And who did I really?

I didn't take long to change, exchanging my dress for a pair of shorts, a tee, and some hiking boots that Matt had gotten me a few years ago when I'd told him I wanted to hike part of the Pacific Crest. I'd never gotten around to it because it was across the country and even a part of it was a serious time commitment, but every time I tied the boots on, I thought about that vision. The possibility of turning a dream into a reality.

Ten minutes later, the elevator doors opened on the first floor to reveal Jacob in the exact spot I'd left him. There wasn't a drink in his hand that hadn't been there before, already half gone. His eyes weren't wandering the scene like they were trained to do. He was staring at the elevator like he hadn't blinked since I'd left.

"I like it. Rugged chic." Jacob motioned at me in my hiking digs, pushing off the wall like he was about to pull me into his arms. He stopped at the last minute, as though he knew I wouldn't welcome it.

"You might want to change too," I suggested when I realized he was wearing a nice pair of shoes and light slacks. "The trail isn't crazy extreme, but it's not an easy one either. Plus, it will probably be muddy and stuff could have fallen onto the trail from the wind."

Jacob glanced out the bank of windows at the entrance. "Yeah, there's this thing known as a tropical storm swirling around us. Maybe not the ideal conditions to be hiking."

I waved it off, zipping up my rain jacket just in case. If nothing else, it would cut the wind. "It's not bad." He fell into step beside me as I moved toward the exit. "Sure you don't want to change?"

His head shook. "I'll be fine. A little dirt won't kill me."

There was a cab waiting for us out front, so after we crawled inside, I told the driver what trail to head to and we took off. I couldn't help staring out the window, hoping to catch a glimpse of Matt. I was eager to get this conversation with Jacob over with for more reasons than just getting answers and deciding where to go from there. I was eager to get it over with so I could get back to Matt. Get back to whatever it had been he was about to say to me.

Because I was pretty sure I knew. Because I was pretty sure I felt the same way, even now, after what had happened over the past few days. Three days. It felt like years instead of days.

Jacob pulled my buckle across my lap when I didn't move to fasten it. Then he reached for my hand slowly, like he was giving me time to pull it away if I didn't want him to hold it. I kept it where it was, letting his hand fold around mine.

"When I found out what happened . . . when I realized what I'd done . . ." He paused, staring out the front windshield. "I wasn't sure if I'd ever see you again."

I twisted in my seat to face him. What the hell? It was as good a time as any to clear the air and finally get some answers. "What did you do?"

He blinked, looking as if he were somewhere else.

"Jacob—"

He motioned at the quiet cab driver, like he was hanging on our every word. Which he really wasn't. Even if he was, I didn't care at this point. I didn't care who heard, just so long as I finally knew why the man I was supposed to marry three days ago didn't show up to the wedding.

"I don't remember." He swallowed, looking like he was choking on an apple. "I don't have a goddamn clue what happened that night or that next day. All I remember was being out with the guys one minute, and the next I was stumbling through Dad's front door, trying to figure out what the hell just happened."

My head turned so it was facing him. "You don't remember? Nothing?"

He looked me in the eye as he said, "Nothing more than what I just told you."

"You mean to tell me that you lost track of a whole twenty-four-hour period? That it's all a blank?" I paused, lifting my eyebrow. "You don't have a single memory of that whole day?"

One of his shoulders shrugged. "I wish I did. I really wish I did, because I can tell it's eating you up. Hell, it's eating me up. I missed my own wedding for Christ's sake."

He blew out a breath and slammed his head back against the headrest. "But if I told you anything else, it would be a lie, and I don't want to lie to you anymore, Cora. Not now that we're married."

The word hit me hard. "We're *not* married. Because you didn't show up."

"Yeah, but we would be. We should be." His fingers tightened around mine as the cab slowed when we pulled into the parking lot for the trailhead. "We kind of are, since Matt had my back and stepped in to do what he did. I know you're pissed at him about that—I am a little too—but he did it for me. He did it for us. Because he knows we're meant to be together. He *knows* that."

Everything about his words, everything on his face, led a person to the impression that he believed with his whole heart what he'd just said. But when he looked away, trying to hide his glare out the window as his hand tightened around mine, I knew the truth. He didn't believe those words any more than I did. At least not completely.

"Does everyone know what happened?" I swallowed, thinking about the rumors that would be flying when I got back to Miami. Rumors had always seemed to follow me wherever I went, from the time I moved into the Adams' place with my mom. Most of them had been untrue, but not all of them.

Jacob's head shook as he paid the driver, leaving him a nice tip. "No, when I showed up and Dad and I started to put the pieces together, he told me not to tell anyone. He basically had me swear on my life not to tell anyone, then to get my ass down here and fix my mistake." He slid out of the cab, holding his hand out for me to take as I came out. "No one knows. No one knew it was Matt. Dad's going to talk to his attorney so we can figure out all of the legal headaches that might be involved, but we'll get this straightened out. It might mean you and I need to have a private ceremony of our own to make it official, but you have my word that I'll fix my mistake and make this right."

My head was nodding, but it was more in recognition of what he was saying than in agreement. When I went to slide my daypack onto my back, Jacob took it.

"Here, I've got it." He adjusted the straps to fit him, clasping the chest strap over his button-down shirt.

Before the cab drove off, Jacob requested he be back in an hour to pick us up like he had a clue how long this hike would take. I stood there observing the man I'd spent ten years of my life committed to. He looked totally different than he had last night—half-drunk, half-crazy, and ready to take on the whole world blindfolded if need be. Today he looked like he'd gotten a full night's rest, his clothes were clean and ironed, his eyes were bright, and his mood was almost carefree. This was the Jacob I remembered as a child.

This was the person I'd fallen in love with—instead of the one I'd been reminding myself I loved lately.

"You lead, I'll follow." Jacob motioned at the trailhead, waiting for me.

I started up the trail at a solid pace, feeling like I needed to burn out the emotions and adrenaline I'd stored up. My legs were on fire when he tapped my arm with a bottle of water.

"Drink. I don't need you getting dehydrated on me." He was breathing a little harder than normal, but not much. Jacob might not have been into hiking, but he stayed fit.

"Are you going to wipe my brow next?" I smiled back at him, taking the water to have a few sips.

"If you want me to." His eyes met mine for a moment as we wound up the trail. "Whatever you want, all you have to do is ask."

My head turned to focus on the trail. "I'd like to have the truth. The *real* reason you missed our wedding."

"I already told you—"

"You remember something," I interrupted. "I've seen you drink a whole fifth of scotch and walk a straight line like it was nothing. You might have been drinking that night—a lot—but you remember something." I took a breath. "I want to know what that something is."

"Cora—"

"No." My head shook. "Just the truth. That's all. That's all I want from you right now. I don't want anything else until I have that."

"Anything else I told you wouldn't be the truth though, baby. Don't you get it? I can't tell you anything but what I remember about that night, and there's nothing I can recall." There was the slightest edge in his voice. I was questioning him—pushing him—and he didn't like it. "What about just the truth from you? That's all I want too. Matt won't say anything—he told me to ask you. And you won't say anything because you're too busy accusing me of something you think I did that I can't remember."

My pace was picking up as the trail grew steeper. My heart was hammering, my lungs straining, my legs burning, but I couldn't slow down. I couldn't stop. I was finally moving forward, and I knew I couldn't stop for fear of never being able to restart again.

"You already know what happened." I glanced over my shoulder; he'd fallen back a few steps but was still following. Jacob's chest was moving fast now too. "You didn't show up. Matt made an impulsive decision, put on your tux, and was the one waiting for me when I walked down that aisle. We said our vows"—I left out the kissing part. Jacob already knew it and hearing me say it would only set him off—"we went to the reception, then St. Thomas. And then the next day, I found out what had happened. *That's* the truth."

I kept moving, knowing that wasn't the *whole* truth. Jacob wasn't naïve enough to believe it was either. He knew something else had happened—he just didn't know to what degree.

"The next morning. You didn't find out that Matt was Matt until the next morning." He let those words simmer in the air. "That means you spent your first night of your honeymoon, as man and wife, doing what? Watching reruns and ordering room service? Holding hands and reading to each other?" Jacob paused, the sarcasm in his voice palpable. "Fucking like a couple of animals until the sun rose?"

My feet broke to a stop. Slowly, I turned around to face him. He didn't stop moving up the trail until he was right in front of me. His eyes met mine and I made sure to look straight in them. "You want to talk to me like that, you'll just have to wait for your precious answers."

My voice was calm, but everything beyond that wasn't. He knew. He could see it in my face or had read it on Matt's or had figured it all out on his own. Jacob knew Matt and I had been together the way any couple would on their wedding night. He knew. Now he just needed to hear me confirm it.

"I'd been drinking. One minute I was awake, and then I woke up the next morning. I don't remember. Sorry." As I fed his words back to him, his jaw ground together, but he stayed quiet. "To tell you anything else would be a lie."

Turning around, I attacked the rest of the trail. I knew I couldn't *not* tell Jacob, but for right now, this would have to do. I wasn't ready to tell him the truth, and from the anger I could imagine dammed up inside him, he wasn't ready to hear it either.

This wasn't the right time. Out here in the middle of some isolated trail, no witnesses, no where to go besides up or down was not the ideal spot for someone to tell their jealous-to-the-extreme fiancé they'd just slept with his brother. Multiple times. And that it had been the best sex of my life—not that I was planning on mentioning that, but still, it was the truth.

My shoulder lifted as I moved. "I just can't remember," I repeated, wondering if he believed those words as much as I had.

"Don't play games with me." His feet scrambled up the trail after me. "Don't lie to me."

When my head whipped back to glare at him, I found him right behind me again. So close his feet were falling into my footprints as soon as I stepped away. "Kind of ironic, isn't it? You accusing me of lying? You accusing me of playing games?"

"What does that mean?"

"You know what that means."

The sky was a swirl of grey, but the wind was just a breeze back here. I couldn't tell if that was because we were sheltered from the storm or if the storm was dying, but it made me hopeful that we'd weather it.

"Enlighten me." Jacob's hand found my wrist, pulling on it to stop me.

My eyes narrowed into slits at him before dropping to where his hand was tied around my wrist. "Let me go."

"Not until you tell me what happened." With his other hand, he found my waist and twisted me around.

My blood felt like lava right then—molten and scorching. "Take your hands off me. Now." I gave him a moment to do so. He didn't. "You want answers, this is the guaranteed way to never get them." I tried to shake his hand off of my waist, but it felt plastered to me. His fingers roped around my wrist felt the same. "Jacob, I'm serious. Take your damn hands off of me."

"Why? You like Matt's on you better?"

My free hand twitched at my side, coming so close to slapping him I could feel the tingle in my palm from the imaginary strike. "Let. Go."

His head shook, his eyes trained on mine. "No."

I pulled against him, but he was as serious about not letting go as his hold was. "Let me go, Jacob."

His fingers only tightened, making my wrist hurt enough I could feel my pulse throbbing in it. "Never."

I could see from the look in his eyes he was talking about something other than just our present situation, but I was not in an understanding mood right then. Since words were getting me nowhere, I pulled against him. It didn't get me far. Using every scrap of strength in my body, I twisted and pulled against him, somehow managing to get free of his hold all at once.

All of my momentum sent me flying backward though, staggering a few steps until the heel of my boot caught on something.

Jacob tried to grab my hand to catch me as I fell—I didn't miss the look that cast over his face as I flew back—

but he couldn't get to me. I had just enough time to try to twist around to break my fall, just getting one hand beneath me when my body crashed into the ground.

A breath rushed out of my lungs from the impact, my body feeling like I'd just collided with a slab of cement instead of compacted earth.

"Cora! Shit! Are you okay?" Jacob slid onto his knees beside where I'd fallen on the trail, his face worried as he scanned my body like he was looking for signs of blood or bones puncturing through the skin.

It had been a hard fall, but not that bad of one.

"I'm fine." My eyes squeezed closed as I started sitting up, my head throbbing from the movement. It wasn't until I'd sat up that I felt one side of my face was hot and wet. When my hand touched my temple, where the pain was resonating from, my fingers came away glazed with blood.

"Your head." Jacob's throat moved. "It's bleeding." His voice was the very embodiment of calm, but his eyes were as uneasy as I'd ever seen them.

"Yeah, I just figured that out," I said, realizing the blood was winding down my face and dripping onto my tank. Great time and place to get a head injury.

"I need to get you to the hospital." Jacob had already taken off my daypack and was unbuttoning his dress shirt. He pulled out of it one arm at a time.

My head shook as I touched at my temple again. Head lacerations bled like crazy. "No, get me to Matt. I don't want to go to a hospital for a few stitches." I guessed it would only take a few, instead of the fifty it seemed from all of the blood flowing from it. "He can take care of me. Just take me back to Matt."

I hadn't realized what I'd said, or how I'd said it, until I looked at Jacob.

"Please? He travels everywhere with the requisite doctor stuff for exactly this kind of thing. I'd rather have him stitch me up than someone I don't know after waiting who knows how long in an emergency room."

Jacob didn't say anything, but he nodded. "If that's what you want, I'll get you back to Matt."

The note of resignation in his voice confused me. I'd expected more anger, but instead I'd found almost the opposite. I'd expected a fight instead of a surrender.

"Don't." My head shook as he gripped the arm of his shirt. "It's your favorite shirt. I've got a bandana in my bag we can use and some gauze in the first aid kit."

Jacob didn't say anything. He just ripped off the sleeve of his shirt. "Yeah, and you're my favorite person. Hell with the shirt."

As he pressed it to my head, I sat still, watching him from the corner of my eye. He looked so worried, like I was droplets away from bleeding out or something. So guilty, like this was his fault.

"It's not your fault, Jacob. I tripped. It's okay—I'll be fine."

He didn't say anything; he just stayed crouched beside me, pressing his shirtsleeve to my temple like he could do it all day without getting tired.

"I need to get you back down to the trailhead," he said, his voice sounding far off. "Can you hold this against your head okay?" He gently lifted my hand and folded it over the shirtsleeve. He was waiting for my answer.

"Think I can muster up the strength somehow." I managed a smile, but he didn't see it. He was too busy snapping up my pack and scooping me into his arms. "What are you doing?"

"Getting you down the trail." His arms curled around me, feeling as strong as they did careful, right before he hoisted me up from the ground.

"Jacob, put me down."

"Not happening." He was already moving down the trail, every step as sure as the one before.

"It's my head that's the problem. My legs are working just fine." I lifted my eyebrows at him, but his focus was aimed on the trail he was moving down especially fast, given he was carrying a grown adult.

"I'm getting you down this thing. In one piece." His hands formed deeper into me. "We can argue about it the whole way down if you want, but I'm not putting you down."

I sighed. "Jacob."

"Not letting go." He glanced at me like he was challenging me to keep pushing him. "But please feel free to keep voicing your protests. You know I like it when you get all bossy on me."

I fought my smile. "I have a serious head wound and you're making jokes?"

He kept his eyes on the trail, but I didn't miss the amusement that washed into them. "Oh, yeah, sure. Now that I'm making jokes, it's a serious head wound. Back there when you were making your plea to walk down on your own, it was a microscopic scratch."

I shook my head, giving a loud enough sigh that he knew I wasn't happy about our present situation, but I was resigned to it. He just grinned at me, like we were playing one of the games we used to play as kids.

We didn't say anything else the rest of the trek down. I hadn't realized how far we'd made it or how long we'd been out, but when the parking lot came into view, the cab was just pulling back in.

"Thank god," Jacob breathed when he saw it.

"Not excited about the idea of schlepping me all the way back to the hotel?" I asked, checking his face for signs of strain. There were none.

"If it meant getting to hold on to you, I'd carry you through the rest of our lives." As soon as he looked down at me, he glanced away. "But I'd rather get you into a vehicle that can travel thirty miles per hour, or forty-five if I promise a really great tip."

The cab driver saw us coming and already had the back door open when we emerged from the trailhead. When he noticed my head, his eyes went round.

"Hospital?" he guessed, already rushing around to the driver seat.

From the way the guy was moving, I guessed it looked like my skull had been split open.

Jacob bit his cheek, waiting for me to answer as he set me down and guided me into the backseat.

"Back to the hotel please," I told the driver.

Jacob didn't say anything; he just pulled his phone out as he slid into the seat beside me. "Give him a call so he's waiting for us when we get there." His eyes stayed forward as I took the phone, punching in Matt's number.

It rang.

It kept ringing.

Then it went to voicemail.

"He didn't answer. I'll leave a message," I whispered, but Jacob slid the phone from my hand.

"Call him on yours."

"But I just tried. He's not answering."

He shifted in his seat as he handed me my daypack. "But he'll answer yours."

Pulling my phone out of the bag, I gave him a doubtful look as I hit the two button Matt's number was saved under.

"My number still in the number one spot?" Jacob was peering at my phone.

"Of course it is," I said as I lifted the phone to my ear.

"Matt's number two?"

I shrugged, wondering why I needed to answer that when he'd just watched me hit two.

"Does that order still extend beyond your speed-dial line-up?" he asked, lifting his head so it was aligned with mine.

I was saved having to answer that loaded question when the phone started to ring. It didn't have a chance to ring twice before the other end clicked.

"Cora?"

I didn't know why, but hearing Matt's voice made me kind of sink into the seat. It made me feel like no matter what was going on, everything was going to be all right in the end. Actually, he'd always made me feel that way. From the first week I'd moved into their house and accidentally broken a vase and he'd helped me clean it up, telling me it would be okay, to right now, years later, when I'd just smashed my head—and possibly my heart—and was calling him for help. Later, I'd found out he'd taken the blame for breaking the vase and been grounded for a week. I'd begged him to tell the truth, but he'd stood firm. So I'd sneaked him dinner every night that week, since grounding in the Adams' house meant going to bed without dinner.

"Cora?" This time his voice was strained.

Beside me, Jacob nudged me, his gaze aimed out the front window.

"Matt, I fell. I think I need stitches—"

"What? Wait. Where are you?" In the background, I heard noise, like he was rushing around.

"I was hiking. I only need a few stitches, I think, and didn't want to go to the hospital if you wouldn't mind—"

"Of course I don't mind. Where are you? I'll meet you there." More rustling around, followed by what sounded like a door slamming.

"We're on our way back to the hotel. Could you meet us back at my hotel room?"

"You're with Jacob?" It went quiet in the background, then Matt's voice changed. "He was with you when you were hiking? When you fell?"

My eyes shifted toward Jacob. I wasn't sure if he could hear what Matt was saying, and his expression gave nothing away. "Yeah, he was with me."

A few beats of silence. "Cora . . ." He exhaled. "Did he—"

"Matt, please. Just meet us back at the hotel. We'll probably be there in another ten minutes."

On the other end, he was silent. I knew Matt so well I knew exactly what he was thinking. Now wasn't the time to try to convince him I'd fallen all on my own.

"I'll be there," he said at last, but the line didn't go dead.

It never did when we were on the phone together—he always waited for me to cut the connection. I wasn't sure why, but I'd tested it out a few years ago. I'd called to check on him when he first started working at the hospital he was at now. He was working all of the time, sleeping more often at the hospital than at his condo, and I'd been worried about him overdoing it. I caught him one night just as he was getting off a shift and crawling into his bed at home. After chatting for a few minutes, we said good-bye, then I waited. The line didn't go dead, just like it didn't now.

I'd watched the clock on my stove for two minutes, and just when I was sure he'd fallen asleep with the phone still tucked to his ear, I said, "Good night, Matt." His response came right after. "Night, Cora." I hung up after that, guessing he'd never be the first.

This time was the same.

After stuffing my phone into my pocket, I chanced a look at Jacob. He was silent beside me, unmoving.

"Hey, I'm okay." I moved the shirtsleeve away from my temple so he could see the bleeding was slowing. "A few stitches and a shower and I'll be good as new."

"No." He had to work his jaw loose. "This is my fault."

I sat forward in my seat, trying to get him to look at me. He wouldn't. "I tripped on my own merit. What do you think is your fault?"

His head turned away from mine. "Everything."

After that, the rest of the ride back was quiet. My head wasn't bleeding nearly as much, but it was throbbing. I wanted to grab the bottle of pain reliever I kept in my backpack for exactly this kind of thing, but the mood in the cab was so somber, I was afraid to move.

When the driver pulled up to the hotel entrance, I let out a sigh, feeling like I'd just survived some kind of challenge. Jacob helped me out and paid the driver, looking like he wanted to carry me inside and through the lobby, but I stopped that by bouncing up the stairs on my own.

The few people inside the lobby gaped at me as I came in. I probably looked like I'd just been an extra in some new slasher movie. Checking out the panel of windows facing the ocean, I noticed the waves looked the same size as they had earlier today. The wind even looked like it had slowed down some.

"Any update on the storm?" I asked the woman at the reception desk.

She smiled and tried not to stare at me like I was a freak show. "It's going to miss us. Looks like we'll just get a bit of wind and a lot of rain probably."

Jacob was waiting beside me, an impatient look on his face, but he wasn't pulling on me to keep going.

"That's good news."

"Isn't that the way it goes? You plan for the worst, hope for the best, and land somewhere in between." The woman cleared her throat, looking away when her eyes shifted to where I still had Jacob's shirtsleeve pressed to my head. "Can I call an ambulance for you, ma'am? Maybe give you directions to the nearest hospital?"

Beside me, Jacob sighed.

I shook my head. "Thanks, but I've got a doctor waiting for me upstairs. He'll take care of me."

The woman nodded as I started toward the elevators, while Jacob stepped in front of me so he could punch the up button. A door was just opening when I approached.

The ride up to my room was just as quiet as the one in the cab here. Although that might have had more to do with both of us knowing Matt was waiting for us a few floors away.

As soon as the doors opened, I practically lunged out into the hall.

Jacob moved up behind me a moment later. "In a hurry?"

I didn't answer that, because I had no good answer to give him. I was in a hurry, and it wasn't to get my head sewn up either.

Matt was already here, leaning into the door of my room, his eyes trained on the elevator like he'd known it was about to open. He wasn't in my room, thank god. He had a key—I'd given him one—but he'd been smart enough not to use it, probably knowing what I did. Jacob would lose it if he found Matt in my room, room key in hand.

Matt started to smile when he saw me. That smile faded when he took a good look at me. Shoving off the door, he moved down the hall a few steps to meet us. "I thought you said you needed a few stitches, not a few hundred and a possible blood transfusion." Matt's messenger bag—which he kept the standard-fare doctor kit in—was slung over his shoulder, and he was already digging through it.

"It's a head wound. They bleed like crazy. You're a doctor—why do I need to tell you this?" I put on my best unconcerned face as Jacob and I moved down the hall, but I had plenty of things to be concerned about. The gash on my head ranked low on that list.

Jacob slid closer to me with every step we took, until our shoulders were brushing by the time we stopped in front of my room. Matt had barely acknowledged Jacob until now. Then Matt covered my hand with his and slowly pulled aside the shirtsleeve to see the extent of the damage.

His face didn't give a thing away—but he was trained not to show any emotion when a patient's guts were spilling out on the floor at his feet. He didn't show any emotion until his fingers gently touched the area around the cut and I winced from the rush of pain that came with it.

Matt's jaw locked up, his eyes darkening before they swiveled toward Jacob. Before the two of them could work that out, fists first, I hurried to pull the room key from my pack and kick the door open the moment the green lights flashed.

"What happened?" Matt snapped at Jacob.

It was me who answered him though. "I fell."

Jacob echoed my response as we all moved inside the room. "She fell."

Matt slid his bag off and set it on the desk, already flipping on lights and starting to grab towels from the bathroom. "Yeah, I got that terribly informative answer on the phone earlier. How about the details? Now that it looks like you *fell* off of a cliff."

I headed into the bathroom as Matt glared at Jacob like this was all his fault. Though I expected a response, Jacob didn't say anything to defend himself. Instead, he stayed quiet, falling into one of the chairs tucked into the corner.

"What do you think you're doing?" Matt asked me when I started to close the bathroom door.

"Taking a quick shower to rinse the blood and dirt off."

"I don't think so. You need to get your head stitched up before your brains start falling out." Matt moved toward the bathroom like he was going to physically sit me down in that chair by the desk if I didn't do it myself.

So I hurried to close the door, knowing there was no way he'd open that door once I'd closed it. Knowing there was no way Jacob would let him either.

I didn't want to leave those two alone for long, so I hurried through the shower as quickly as possible. Only a few minutes later, I emerged from the steam-filled bathroom with a towel twisted around my hair and wearing a swimsuit cover-up I'd had hanging in the bathroom.

The brothers looked like they'd spent a few years in some foreign prison though. Their expressions were hardened, their eyes blank, every muscle in their body looking trigger-pin ready for action.

"Wow. This isn't a funeral, boys. Just a few stitches and a little loss of blood."

Matt huffed over my "little" word choice. When Matt's face, which had been trained on the ground, lifted, his eyes met mine, which were aimed on him. Not Jacob. Him. The corner of his mouth twitched, but he tamed his smile. Probably a good idea since Jacob was watching him, his hands braced around the chair's armrests like he was capable of ripping them off.

Suddenly, Matt's face changed, his gaze sweeping a bit lower. Pushing off the desk, he grabbed one of the towels from his collection and started toward me. Jacob rose from his chair but stayed where he was.

Matt shook out the towel, blocking me from Jacob's view, then draped the towel over my shoulder. Subtly, his gaze lowered to the spot on my chest just above the barrier of my cover-up where a slightly bruised red mark was showing. The same mark he'd given me here in my hotel room, when I'd known exactly who he was when I put my hands on him.

"Wouldn't want you ruining another piece of clothing," he said in a normal voice, shooting me a wink as he tucked the towel down a little lower.

Behind him, I could make out Jacob starting to pace, moving closer with every turn. He didn't like Matt being so close to me. He didn't like Matt talking to me or touching me or being the only one who could help me in this instance.

When Matt tucked the towel back from my temple a bit more, his jaw set as he inspected my cut again. "Take a seat. That's going to require more than a couple stitches, but I'll go as quickly as I can." He pulled the desk chair out for me then adjusted the table lamp so it was aimed in my direction. "Here, take a few of these."

He shook a few pain relievers into my hand and handed me a bottle of water after I'd tossed them into my mouth. Jacob came around beside us, still pacing as he watched the scene like he was helpless.

Matt didn't seem to notice Jacob as he pulled things out of his messenger bag, his hands moving with the kind of speed and precision only a surgeon's would, I guessed. I had a flash of what those hands felt like on me, and my body instantly reacted to it. I had to shift in my seat and look away from Matt and his hands to keep from blushing in front of both of them.

"How did you fall?" Matt asked, rolling up his sleeves as he started for the bathroom to wash his hands. His gaze cut to Jacob when neither of us said anything right away.

"I fell backward. My heel caught on a rock or a root or something," I said, waiting for him to come back, hoping he'd believe it was as simple as that. From the look on his face when came out of the bathroom, he didn't.

Matt's hand gently tipped my head back against the chair, turning it so my cut was facing him. Jacob rolled his head a few times, popping his neck.

"You make a habit of hiking backward?" Matt's brow carved into his forehead as he cleaned the cut. Every time I cringed from the sting, he winced with me.

"Sometimes. When I'm feeling crazy."

"Are you going to tell me what really went down, or leave me to fill in the blanks?"

I wasn't sure if he was talking because he really wanted to know that badly or as a way to distract me from what he was doing, especially now that he was starting to numb the area around my gash. Needles and I weren't exactly simpatico, as Matt had figured out years ago when I'd come back from my eleven-year-old doctor appointment feeling like a pincushion and looking like I'd just been through hell. Ever since, he'd come with me to all of my doctor appointments that involved needles, from blood draws to my annual flu vaccine. He found some new way to distract me each time, either by running some funny video on his phone or making faces at me.

As my silence stretched into the next minute, Matt glanced at Jacob, waiting for an answer.

Jacob lifted his chin. "I don't know. Are either of you going to eventually tell me what 'really went down' on this island before I got here, or is swept under the rug going to be the way of all of it?"

"Not the time, Jacob. Not the right damn time." Matt's head turned back toward me, the skin between his brows deepening as he finished numbing my temple. To his credit, I barely felt a thing after the first initial poke.

"I don't know. We're all three here, not going anywhere too soon. Seems like the right damn time to me." When Jacob looked over Matt's shoulder to see what was happening, his forehead creased, remorse filling his face before he had a chance to turn away. "You two had separate rooms, right?"

Matt's teeth ground together, his mouth staying shut as he disposed of the needle and gathered what he needed to sew me up.

"That's right," I answered, figuring this was about as basic of a question as I could expect from Jacob on this topic.

Jacob rolled his head again. "Yeah, except I checked with the front desk and this room wasn't checked out until the second night." He turned so he was angled toward me. "So that means you must have both shared the cabin."

"The first night we did." Matt came into the conversation then, his voice as even as I'd ever heard it. His eyes flickered to mine once, something in them telling me it would be okay. It might have been foolhardy and naïve, but I believed him. Somehow, Matt found a way to make everything okay. "It was late. I took the couch."

Jacob nodded, his gaze wandering from Matt to me, like we somehow had every answer he was looking for. "Was this before or after Cora knew you were you?"

"What the hell does that matter?" Matt's head turned over his shoulder, a lethal expression forming.

Jacob lifted his shoulder as he backed into the wall behind him. "Because it does. Say you guys got it on but Cora thought you were me—she's not to blame. I can forgive her for wanting to have sex with her husband on their wedding night." His nostrils flared as he sucked in a breath. "But I will kill you, Matt, if you put your hands on her like that. I will end you if you fucked her when she thought she was with me."

The corners of Matt's eyes creased as he set the first stitch. Again, I barely felt a thing—even when he was doing something painful, it was impossible for Matt to hurt me.

"So you'd prefer the possibility that we made love knowing exactly who the other was?" Matt asked.

Jacob shoved off the wall, his eyes blazing. "Tell me. Look me in the eyes and tell me. I'm tired of you messing with me. Smirking in my face. Strutting around like you screwed my girl."

Matt was taking slow, purposeful breaths. That was the only indication he gave that Jacob was getting to him. The whole time, his hands never wavered, his gaze intent, his whole façade focused.

"I'm a little busy stitching up *your girl*." He didn't pull his tone as he continued. "That 'looking you in the eye and telling you what either did or didn't happen' thing is going to have to wait."

"Fine. Don't look me in the eye. Just tell me." Jacob had managed to wrestle himself back against the wall, but his body was twitching from what I guessed was adrenaline and emotion.

"You're making an awful lot of assumptions. Throwing around a lot of accusations at the person you say you love most in the world." Matt kept working, not blinking as he fixed me.

"I don't *say* I love her most in the world. I *do* love her most in the world."

"Of course you do. You make that clear every single day. Like the day you didn't make it to your wedding. And the day after that, when you showed up and accused her of screwing me behind your back. You don't have to convince me of your profound love for Cora. Consider me sufficiently convinced."

My breath caught in my chest as I looked at Matt. He was too focused on my temple to meet my stare, but I wasn't sure what he would have read in my eyes if he had. Part of me felt like I was telling him to stop, another felt like I was telling him to keep going—to never stop.

Jacob's hands were curling into fists, releasing, then forming again a moment later. "Keep talking and I'm not going to need you to tell me what happened. I'm going to figure it out all on my own."

"Seems like you think you've already got all the answers."

"Enough." My voice projected through the room louder than I'd intended. "Both of you." This time when I glanced at him, Matt's eyes met mine for a beat. "This male bravado crap isn't helping anything." Jacob stuck his arm out toward Matt like he was to blame, but I kept going. "Jacob, I'll answer all of your questions that I can. What I can't remember, I can't help you with. Kind of like you can't help me with what you don't remember."

Jacob was the first to look away, his jaw straining through his skin.

"We've all been through a hell of a few days, and maybe we all just need a little time to figure out what happened and what comes next." I didn't realize my hand was moving toward Matt until I felt it brush his shirt.

Jacob didn't see it, but Matt didn't miss it. He leaned in a little closer, until my hand connected with his body hidden beneath his shirt. My fingers curved into his stomach before falling back into my lap. Jacob couldn't see, but that didn't mean it was right for me to be touching his brother with him ten feet away.

"I'm with Cora," Matt said, blowing at a chunk of hair that had fallen over his forehead.

"Big surprise there," Jacob muttered.

"Need a little help?" I smiled when Matt blew another hard breath, only to result in another chunk of hair falling into his face.

"Please. This is why those head wraps are so convenient in surgery. Wouldn't want to accidently sever an artery trying to get hair out of my eye."

When my smile went higher, Jacob's shoulders tensed. Taming it as best as I could, I lifted my hand to slide Matt's hair back into place. The whole time I was touching him, Jacob looked like he was fighting every instinct inside him to stay where he was, while Matt looked like he was heeding every instinct inside him by staying where he was—facing me, his back exposed to his enemy.

"Better?" I asked.

One corner of his mouth lifted. "Better."

Another minute passed, this one in silence. From the feel of it, Matt was almost done. I wasn't sure if I was happy about that or not, because what came next? Where did the three of us go from here? We were all stuffed into this small hotel room, but what would happen when the last stitch was sewed into place? Would Matt go? Would he stay? Would we talk, or would we need to think?

Either way, I knew I'd be leaving this island in a few days. I just wasn't sure who I'd be leaving with. Or if I'd be leaving all alone.

"Why did you fall?" Matt asked, shattering the silence.

When I shifted in my seat, Jacob stepped in. "We were talking."

"About what?" From the flash in Matt's eye, he already knew.

"I was asking her about you two," Jacob answered. "Since neither one of you are volunteering too much information and I need to know. I have a right to know."

Matt's eyes darkened, his shoulders tense. "She fell because you were having a fight?"

"I fell because I tripped," I interjected, hoping Matt would hear the plea in my voice that was asking him to let it go and move on.

"I didn't push her. I've never laid a hand on her like that." Jacob pushed off the wall, his arm flying between him and me like the idea was absurd. When Matt stayed quiet, refusing to accept what had just been said, Jacob's face went red. "How dare you. You think I'd put my hands on Cora? That I could hurt her like that?"

His footsteps sounded like thunder rolling in the distance as he moved toward us, but Matt never once looked over his shoulder. I wondered if he was banking on the assumption that Jacob wouldn't charge when I was close by, or maybe Matt just didn't care if he got blindsided by his brother.

"You've hurt her in every other way, right?" Matt paused just long enough for that to charge the still air. "But if you did, if you did physically hurt her, that ending favor will be returned, brother."

Matt must have been finished with my stitches because his hands lowered at his sides, the skin between his brows deepening as he inspected my temple. It was eerie how calm he was, how in control of his emotions and body he could be when his twin had never looked so close to losing his grip. With the way Jacob was looking, and the way I knew Matt was feeling, I knew the moment Matt stepped away from me, Jacob would charge.

"He hasn't," I said, looking at Matt as he started to rise. "He didn't. I wouldn't be with him if he had. That's not the type of person I want to spend my life with."

I'd been so focused on saying the right thing to calm them both down just enough to keep a fight from ensuing, I didn't realize what I'd actually said.

Or how it would be taken.

Matt's eyes narrowed as he started putting everything back in his bag. He wouldn't look at me. "You wouldn't be with him," he said slowly, repeating my words. "That's not the type of person you want to spend your life with."

His hands braced against the desk after he'd packed up the last of his things. A sharp exhale popped out of his mouth as he shook his head. When he did finally look at me, it wasn't the same Matt I'd spent the past few days with. It was someone else. A shell of that person.

"Thanks for the reminder. I needed it. I'll leave you two alone." He threw his bag across his shoulder, leaving the bottle of pain relievers on the desk in front of me.

As he started for the door, his name was rising from my throat.

Jacob stepped in front of him. "I need to know." Jacob didn't look as wild as before, but he still looked dangerous.

Matt's entire back went rigid. "You want to know what happened?" I didn't recognize his voice. From the look on Jacob's face, neither did he. "I stepped in and took care of her for you. Again. And just like always, I do all the work and you reap the damn reward." Matt's arm thrust back at where I was still sitting in the chair, stitched up and frozen in place.

I was waiting for him to look at me. I was waiting for him to notice the look in my eyes. The one that would tell him everything he needed to know. The truth I was starting to accept had been a part of me for years, but one I'd chosen to keep hidden from view.

"What are you talking about?" Jacob crossed his arms, stepping in front of Matt again when he tried to go around him. "When have you ever done that?"

Matt was quiet, staring at Jacob like they were having a silent conversation. Growing up with them, I knew that, as twins, they were well-versed with those silent conversations.

"You know when," Matt said, his voice just barely trembling. "You know it. And I know it. And Cora's about to find out if you keep pushing me. You're losing points, so you might want to hang on to the few you still have. Now get out of my way." Matt shoved Jacob aside, hard enough he stumbled back into the wall. "I'm tired of you standing in my way."

CHAPTER SIXTEEN

Cora

Just when I thought things couldn't get worse, there I was holding a bag of ice to my temple, where I'd earned thirteen stitches, sitting in an empty hotel bed and staring at a blank television screen after chasing off one brother by hurting him and the other by shoving him out of my room.

Jacob hadn't been eager to leave. He'd wanted to talk, but I knew what he wanted to talk about and that was still not a conversation I was ready to have. Not until I knew for sure. Not until I'd considered the consequences and was prepared for the fallout.

Matt had taken off, and while I guessed he was back in his cabin, I knew he didn't want to see me. Not after what I'd said. I might not have meant it in the way he'd taken it, but I hadn't said or, more importantly, done anything to show him otherwise.

I needed to know exactly how I felt and get good and comfortable with it before I approached either of them. All three of our lives had been changed when Matt stepped up to that altar. Or going back a little further, our lives had been changed when Jacob didn't show up. Or going farther back still, our lives had been changed the first day we'd all met, three lives weaving together, somehow tangling into an unwieldy knot over the course of twenty years.

My head was still throbbing, a few bruises starting to splotch my skin from the fall, as I stared at that blank television screen and saw what felt like my whole life story play before me. Seeing their life stories unfold along with mine. Matt and Jacob were such a part of my life, they were woven into the very person I was today. They were both a part of me and they always would be, but I could only pick one to spend my life with. One to share a life with, and the other to sever ties with.

I knew that was inevitable. It was the only way it could be after everything. I couldn't choose one and still be friends with the other. That might have worked for the past decade, but it wouldn't work after this. I also knew that might have been due to the brother my conscience had already silently chosen. He might have been okay with a friendship while his brother got more, but it wouldn't work the other way around.

When the knock sounded at my door, I instantly checked the time on my phone. I'd kept it in my lap all evening, hoping it would ring or Matt would send me a message or something to know he hadn't walked through the last door in my life.

It was after nine. Jacob had said he was going to hit the gym and grab dinner after. He'd said he'd swing me up something if I wanted, but I knew what that dinner would come with a side of—more questions. He'd told me to call him if I needed anything, that he'd be five minutes or less away, but he'd promised to give me space.

Sliding out of bed, I grabbed my bathrobe and tied it on. After Jacob finally left, I'd pulled the towel off my shoulder and stood in front of the mirror for a long time, staring at the mark resting above my breast. It looked like a flower just starting to blossom. I stared at it until I could almost feel Matt's mouth on me again, pulling at my skin, taking a part of me and leaving a part of him behind.

Doing a quick check in the mirror, I made sure the bathrobe was covering the mark before I checked the peephole. The person standing on the other side of the door was not who I was expecting. Kind of the last person I was expecting, given her allegiance to the brother I'd just hurt in a way I'd never intended.

My fingers froze on the door handle. I could just pretend I wasn't here. She'd go away eventually. Maggie Stevenson and I had never been friends by any stretch of the word. We'd been more like silent adversaries through high school, then avoided each other as much as possible ever since. She was Matt's friend. I was Matt's friend. By transitive means, that should have made us friends, instead of the opposite.

"I came here to say something to you. So if you don't want to open the door, that's cool. I have no problem saying what I need to right here in the hallway." Maggie's volume was growing with every word. "For everyone to hear."

Sighing, I resigned myself to *this* conversation. When I opened the door, I found her standing there, brows peaked, holding a bottle of champagne in one hand and a couple of paper cups in another.

"Surprise. It's nice to see you too." She smirked at me and what I guessed was my expression at the moment. Then she slid past me into the room.

"What are you doing here?" I asked, cutting to the chase.

She was here for a reason, not to shoot the shit, and the sooner we hashed it out, the sooner I could get back to hashing everything else out. Plus, Maggie didn't do bullshit. She told it like it was. It was one of the things I respected about her. It was also what intimidated me about her.

"I'm here to have a little woman-to-woman talk with you." She waved the bottle in the air before setting it on the desk and giving the bandage covering my temple a curious look. "And I brought my little friend, Dom Perignon, because if this chat goes according to plan, I'm going to be drinking the shit out of this stuff while I celebrate."

Closing the door, I stayed where I was. "Celebrate what?"

"A good friend's happily ever after. Finally," she added, looking at me standing there in my bathrobe, my hair a limp, tangled mess, like she was trying to figure me out.

"Does Matt know you're here?" I asked, crossing my arms.

"No. Matt definitely does not know I'm here." Maggie kicked off her sandals and plopped down onto the end of the mattress, tucking her leg beneath her. "He wouldn't approve if he did, and I can tell from your warm smile that you don't approve, but I'm tired of this evasive shit going on between you two. I'm saying what I need to, once and for all."

"It's never seemed like you had a problem saying what you needed to." I moved into the room and paused at the desk.

Maggie had never pulled her words when she'd been firing them at me or anyone else. Whenever she'd had occasion to go at me, it had always had something to do with Matt. She'd always accused me of doing things to hurt him or lead him on, like I spent my whole existence plotting ways to bring Matt Adams to his knees. What I'd never told her was that I felt the same, but the other way around. It seemed like Matt was coursing his life from one hurting-me moment to the next leading-me-on moment.

"I didn't say half of what I wanted to say to you back then. But I'm about to say it all now, no matter what you or Matt think about it."

"He doesn't want you here because he doesn't want you to say what you came here to tell me, right?" I dropped into the same desk chair Matt had set me in to fix me up. It didn't feel the same without him crouching in front of me though.

"You don't have a clue what I'm here to tell you. Neither does he." Maggie's voice was muffled from the hair tie she'd stuck into her mouth as she remade her ponytail.

I had a guess. One I'd been going back and forth between, but what had to be the only possibility after everything. "Matt. You're here to tell me that he doesn't want me. Not like, beyond this week."

I swallowed, my gaze diverting out the dark windows. Matt might have harbored some feelings for me, some deep-seated desires, but he'd fulfilled them all that night he'd taken me into his bed. Whatever fascination he'd had with me had been realized, and while his friendship would be there for me whenever I needed it, there was nothing hiding behind that designation. Nothing that ran deeper.

"He doesn't like me, does he?" I asked.

Maggie made a face like my words were insulting her. "He doesn't like you?"

My eyes connected with hers for a brief moment. "Not in the way you know I'm talking about."

She shook her head, blinking a few times like she was waking up. "Hi, welcome to planet Earth," she said in a mock cheery voice, waving in my direction. "The place where brains and sound-thinking make the planet go round."

My eyes lifted. "What? I know he has feelings for me, just not the same kind or to the same degree as mine."

"Okay, back up. That, right there." Maggie's finger stabbed in my direction. "That's what I want to delve deeper into. *Your* feelings for *him*. We'll get to his feelings for you in a minute. First, spill. Your guts. Your feelings. Your heart. I want it, right here, scattered on the floor in front of me for my viewing pleasure." Maggie motioned at the floor with a grand flourish, waiting.

I didn't know what to say. Where to start, or how to even start. How did a person sum up a lifetime of emotions in a handful of words? How could I define it to someone else when I had yet to explain it to myself?

"Come on. What's going through that pretty little head of yours? Right this very moment." Maggie scooted forward on the bed, circling her hand like she was trying to encourage me on.

"A lot," was the only way to answer that question.

"I bet. Thought you were marrying one brother only to find out you married the other, who you're starting to finally realize you love too." She paused, giving me a chance to challenge her. I didn't. She smiled. "The upside to this whole cluster of fuck is that either way, you'll wind up Mrs. Cora Adams."

I threw my head back over the headrest, grumbling, "I'm so confused. I've been confused about how I felt about them for years, but now. . ." I came up short, searching for the right word. I wasn't sure there was a right word in the human language for what I was feeling.

"That's not confusion you're warring with when it comes to Matt." Maggie's voice was the gentlest I'd ever heard it as she leaned toward me. "It's knowing how you feel, but believing you shouldn't feel that way. That's different. Being afraid to admit the truth isn't the same as not knowing it."

My breath came out all at once. "I know."

"So you like him?" she asked, adding, "In the way you know I'm talking about?"

My eyes met hers. I nodded.

Her hand compacted into a fist as she drove her elbow back like she was celebrating. "Do you love him?"

I hadn't expected her to ask that. I hadn't been bracing for that word. It was a big one, possibly the biggest one on the planet.

"Hey, I spilled my guts." I waved at the floor between us. "Now it's time to get to the part about how he feels about me." I wasn't saying anything else until she gave something up. I guessed she knew, or had some idea, how Matt felt about me. They'd spent god only knows how many hours at that beach bar talking about whatever they had been. She knew if Matt wanted more from me or if he'd taken all he wanted.

A minute went by, the slowest minute of my life.

Then her eyes found mine. "You *know* how he feels about you." Her head tipped. "Deep down, somewhere inside, you've always known."

"But—"

"You know," she interrupted, her words slow and strong. "Don't fool me. Don't fool yourself. You know. Your heart knows. It just hasn't gotten around to convincing the rest of you."

Everything started to close in around me until life seemed impossibly clear because I could see everything making it up. It wasn't the big picture I'd been waiting for; it was the microscopic details. It wasn't thinking about the past two decades I'd known Matt; it was remembering every day, all of the moments that had made up those nearly twenty years.

"Why didn't he . . . ?" I started, failing to finish my thought. "He never said anything. Never gave me any indication that he might —"

"Feel the same way as you?"

My hands wrung in my lap. "Yeah. I wasn't pretending with Jacob. I did care for him. I *do* care for him. Just with Matt . . . he was a gamble."

"You were with Jacob. Matt thought that's what you wanted." She stood up from the bed and wandered into the bathroom. When she came out, she was carrying a few tissues. I didn't know I'd started crying until she placed them in my lap. "He put what he wanted aside so you could have what you wanted. Or what you seemed to want."

"Yeah?" I dabbed at my face, wondering if there was any end to the mess I'd made in these brothers' lives. I was starting to doubt if there was.

"If you find me someone who's willing to play second-string for years, being the friend while his brother takes all the credit, then swoops in to save the day when I've never needed a hero more, I will auction off all of my non-essential internal organs to the highest bidder."

She was trying to make me smile or laugh or lighten up, but I felt buried under the avalanche of realizations still tumbling down on me. "But Jacob . . . we've been together for years. We were supposed to get married. I'm still wearing the engagement ring he gave me . . . attached to the wedding ring his brother put on my finger." My head shook as I stared at the rings on my finger. "How messed up is that?"

I guessed Maggie would have loved to answer that question for me. She would have accompanied it with a detailed outline and PowerPoint presentation with proven research as to how perfectly and thoroughly messed up I was. For whatever reason, she was staying quiet though.

"Why do you love Jacob?" she finally asked, her face giving nothing away.

My forehead creased. "Because I do."

"Yeah"—she fired me a mock smile—"gonna need to give me more than that, sunshine. Let's try something else. What has he done for you that's made you think, *Damn, that's why I love that man.* The big stuff. What really stands out? He's done something to earn your love, right?" From the note of doubt in her voice, I guessed she wasn't totally convinced.

But I was. Jacob had done things to earn my love. I wouldn't have been with him if he hadn't, especially with the way the past few years had tested every level of our foundation.

"My birthday always fell the week before school started, and Jacob, Matt, and their dad always took that week to vacation in Cabo. I never got to go because it was some guys' trip where they fished and smoked cigars and did whatever else guys do." Maggie and I wrinkled our noses at the same time, imagining it. "But every year, flowers always arrived at the front door, every hour on the hour, nine o'clock in the morning to nine at night. I think it was his way of showing me he wished he could be there when he couldn't be. His way of making me feel special." I thought about my last birthday, how the flowers had shown up at work for me instead since I'd been working a long shift.

Across from me, Maggie was quiet. Too quiet. "Anything else?"

I shifted. "There was the time I had my appendix out and had to miss a ton of school. Jacob collected my homework from each of my classes everyday, completed it *for* me, and turned it all in. I didn't know about it until I returned and got back all of these assignments I hadn't completed. He never said anything—he wasn't looking for any credit. He just did it for me."

Still quiet, Maggie cleared her throat. "Dare I ask if there's anything else?"

My mind flitted to a certain night years ago, the year we'd all been sophomores and gone to the first party of the year at one of Jacob's lacrosse friends' houses. It was a night I didn't think about often. It was also the same night I knew I could, or that maybe I already did, love Jacob Adams.

"Nothing?" Maggie prompted.

There were other things I could have mentioned, but they paled in comparison to what Jacob had done for me that night. Everything in my life could have changed during a handful of moments if it hadn't been for him. Stepping in when he had. Carrying me away from that place how he had.

My whole life could have taken an abrupt detour from that one moment, but it didn't.

"There was a party one night. Our sophomore year." I tried to recount the night without reliving it. I'd never shared the story with anyone, and I wasn't sure I wanted to right now, but she'd asked me why I loved Jacob. This was the catalyst for why.

"Jeremy Penchant's party. First weekend after school started." There wasn't a question in her voice; it was like she'd read my mind.

"That's right. It was my first time drinking, and it didn't exactly agree with me."

"I remember. The tables still remember the scrape of your heels, I'm sure." Maggie pursed her lips.

"You were there?"

She nodded once. "I was there."

"I went with Matt and Jacob, but they were hanging over my shoulder like overprotective big brothers, so I managed to sneak away from them so I could actually mingle with other people."

"And dance on tables," Maggie added.

"Like I said, heavy-handed screwdrivers and sixteen-year-old drinking novice Cora Matthews did not get along well."

"Oh, it looked like the two of you got along really, really well." Maggie eyed the sofa table like she was reliving the scene.

"A while later, post table dancing, I found myself in a room alone. It was dark, there was a bed, and I was so tired. I felt like I just needed a nap and I'd feel better." I had to stop there, waiting for my courage to catch up to my words. "One minute I'm falling asleep, and the next I wake up to the sound of someone in the room with me. Heavy breathing, the sound of clothes being taken off. The feel of someone trying to take off my clothes." My back quaked, but I kept going.

That night had been almost a decade ago, but I still remembered everything about it. From the smell of the musky cologne he'd been wearing, to the way his hands had been clammy and rushed.

"It didn't get far before Jacob found me. He hit the guy once, knocked him out, then carried me out of there. He took me home, put me into bed, and essentially saved me from something that could have changed me forever." I sat up straighter in my chair, making myself look Maggie in the eye. I was surprised to find her eyes glassy. I hadn't thought Maggie Stevenson capable of tears. "The next morning when I woke up and remembered what had happened, that's when I realized I loved him. He'd saved me. Protected me. Taken care of me. He'd shown me what love was, instead of just trying to convince me of it."

Maggie sniffed as she shifted on the bed. "And did your hero ask you anything about it the next day?"

"No, not directly. He asked if I was okay. If I needed anything. But when I didn't bring it up, I think he realized I didn't want to talk about it. I wanted to forget it."

Maggie's hand lifted. "So let me just stop you there." Her eyes narrowed like she was trying to decide what to say next. "Every reason you just listed, every reason you gave me that you have for loving Jacob, is misplaced." She leaned forward, clasping her hands. "It wasn't Jacob. The birthday flowers, the homework, saving you that night—it wasn't him. Every reason you think you love Jacob is really because of Matt."

Whatever she saw on my face made her stop talking. I guessed it was her way of giving me a chance to catch up to what she'd just said.

"What are you talking about? That was Jacob."

She barked out a laugh. "Please. Does Jacob really seem like the flower type of guy? And doing a couple weeks' worth of someone else's homework? He couldn't even get his finished on time."

My mind felt like it was being invaded by an army of conquerors. Everything

I thought I'd known, everything I'd believed, suddenly seemed to be false.

"That night? For sure?" The words came out as a whisper as I tried to remember the face that had shoved through that bedroom door. Everything was so hazy thanks to the alcohol. "How do you know?"

Maggie inhaled. "Because Matt told me."

"He told you?" My throat ran dry as I wondered what else about that night I didn't know or couldn't remember. "Were you there? Did you see anything? Did you see the guy?"

Maggie gave me a sympathetic look before rising to head back into the bathroom. This time she emerged with a glass of water. "No, I wasn't there. I didn't see anything or him. But I know who it was." She stopped in front of me, waiting for me to take the glass.

My arms couldn't move though—nothing could. "How?"

"Because Matt found out who it was—some guy from another school."

My heart felt like it could explode from how fast it was going. "Why would he tell you and not me?"

Maggie didn't settle back onto the edge of the bed. She wandered to the window, staring out it with her arms crossed. "Because I guess he had some talk with you that next morning and kind of inferred that you never wanted to talk about anything related to that night ever again."

She glanced back at me, expecting an argument. She wouldn't get one from me. I hadn't wanted to ever think, let alone talk, about that night. As hard as it had been tonight, it would have been impossible when I was sixteen.

"But he wasn't going to let the guy just get away with it either," she said.

"When he told me he was going to call the cops and tell them he walked in on this asshole undressing some girl he didn't know, I might have suggested an idea."

When she didn't say anything else, I swiveled in my chair so I was angled toward her. "An idea?"

She shrugged, turning around to face me. "That I could be that girl," she said as though it were obvious. "There was no way that guy was going to serve any time without the actual victim testifying, so, voila, I became the victim."

My mouth fell open. "You lied in a court of law?"

Maggie's eyes rolled. "It wasn't a court of law. It was a couple of police officers who took my testimony, along with Matt's."

I gave her a look, waiting for the punch line. There had to be one, right? Matt was really Jacob that night. She pretended to be me. There was a perfectly logical solution to it all—she was messing with me.

When she stood there, straight-faced and silent, my hands drew to my mouth. "Oh my god. You're serious."

"Damn straight I'm serious," she said, pointing at me. "And don't look at me like that. What I did was put a would-be rapist behind bars for a few weeks so he could hopefully reflect on what he'd done and think twice before trying it again. I didn't lose any sleep over it, that's for damn sure."

My world felt like it was crumbling around me—at the same time it felt as though it were all coming together. She wasn't lying. I could see that in her eyes. I could feel it in my bones. This had happened, and I was finally finding out the truth almost a decade later.

"Why didn't he say anything? Why didn't he tell me he found me instead of letting me believe it was Jacob?" I whispered, rising from the chair because I couldn't keep still any longer.

"You didn't want to talk about it. You wanted to put it behind you." She motioned at me, sighing. "And he wanted whatever you wanted."

Now I was the one pacing, trying to figure out what this all meant. What I had to do now. "Why tell me after keeping it a secret for so long?"

Maggie leaned into the windowsill, giving me a sad smile. "Because you deserve to know the truth. And he deserves the damn credit for once in his life." She looked at me like she was waiting for me to acknowledge that. "He's the one, Cora. The real goddamn deal. Don't let him go because you feel guilty or think you should do the right thing or anything stupid like that. Be with the person you want to be with. Stop wasting time."

Everything that had been out of focus for the past few days, for the past ten years, suddenly seemed clear. I had the answers I needed; now I just needed the courage to confront them.

"Thank you." I stopped moving, kind of wanting to give her a hug but kind of knowing she might go *Kill Bill* on me if I tried. "For doing that for me. For being brave when I wasn't."

Maggie's response was a simple shrug, like it was no big deal. "It wasn't just for you. It was for women everywhere who might wind up drinking a little too much and dancing really, really poorly on tabletops."

As her smile moved into place, so did mine.

"It was for him. Matt, who would do anything for you. In case you haven't figured that out yet." Her gaze dropped to my left hand, where the ring on it felt suddenly very heavy. Like it was a weight that would carry me down and eventually drown me if I didn't find some way to be free of it. "And for the record, I believe you love Jacob. Hell, I even believe the selfish asshole loves you. But love is not enough. It isn't." Her head whipped so hard that as she shook it, half of her ponytail fell out again. "Not when it comes to the person you want to spend your life with. You need trust, and sacrifice, and friendship and loyalty and a shit-ton of other stuff." She stopped listing things off on her fingers to stab her finger at me. "Love is not enough. That's a lie. And you know it."

Fresh tears were winding down my face, but I didn't use the tissues to wipe them away. I was tired of hiding my emotions. Exhausted from disguising my feelings. "How do you know I believe that?"

"Because you know the difference." Her expression called me out, knowing she had me.

"Yeah, I do," I said as I slid the ring off of my finger. Whatever the wedding meant, wherever that left the three of us, I knew one thing. "Matt. He's the difference."

Maggie kind of fell into the desk chair, like she'd just drained the last of her energy. "You have no idea how many years I've waited for you to say that," she hollered, stomping her feet on the floor. Her eyebrows bounced, a huge smile in place. "We poppin' the champagne now?"

"Not yet," I said, already backing toward the door. I didn't bother with shoes or changing—I'd lost enough time as it was. "I have things to do first. I have two people I owe a couple of explanations to."

"You might want some champagne in your system for that," Maggie suggested as I pulled the door open.

"Got anything stronger?" I teased, pausing outside the door.

"Not on me." She patted her pockets. "I downed the last mini bottle on the elevator ride up to get me through this talk."

Before I left, I paused. "Thanks, Maggie. For everything you did before, and everything you've done just now."

She made a face, like she'd done nothing. "Hey, you need a wing-woman?" she called as the door started to shut behind me.

"I'd love one, but I have to do this one on my own."

Then I started down the hall, feeling like I was taking the first step in a new life.

CHAPTER SEVENTEEN

Matt

My life. My fucking life.

It was so entwined with hers, I couldn't tell what was me and what was her anymore.

It was like trying to untangle a ball of yarn the size of the Empire State Building without having a clue as to where the end was sticking out. If there was an end to begin with, because it didn't feel like there was. It felt like an unending loop, no end and no beginning, when I thought about my life with Cora.

If that was true, I was going to have to create one. I needed to take a knife and cut through the tangled mess if I had any hope for a somewhat normal life after this.

After marrying my brother's fiancée. After saying "I do" to the woman I'd spent the better part of my life loving from a distance. After experiencing her body and sharing mine with her. After her choosing him all over again.

Some people claimed people like Cora would be the death of them. I knew better though. Death would be a relief contrasted to the next fifty years of life spent without her.

I wished she'd be the death of me already, because I wasn't sure I wanted my life if it meant not having her in it. In some way. In any way. I'd learned not to be picky when it came to time with her.

If I stared at that damn ceiling for a minute more, thinking about her, I was going to lose my mind. Rolling up in bed, I checked the time. It was as dark outside as it was inside my cabin, which meant it had gotten late. It was almost ten. More than eight hours had passed since I walked out of her hotel room, leaving her with the Adams brother she'd chosen. Again. I shouldn't have been surprised; it wasn't anything new. I shouldn't have felt so damn wronged—I was the one who'd set this whole train wreck into motion when I shrugged into Jacob's tux.

She hadn't come looking for me. She hadn't called. She hadn't sent a message. She hadn't wanted me.

Big fucking surprise.

What did I expect? I'd always been Plan B in her life, and after how I'd lied to her with the whole groom-swap thing, why would she have any reason to pick me over Jacob?

The devil you knew was better than the one you didn't.

That was what I kept telling myself as I checked my email on the off chance she'd written me a lengthy message instead. Nothing.

It confirmed my decision to book a flight out of there tomorrow. She might be confused about what had happened between us, but she knew the way she felt about Jacob. This battle for her would end the same as the rest—I'd lose.

A knock on the cabin door shook me from my thoughts. I knew three people on this island at present, but I guessed only one of them would be standing outside my door right now. She was probably here to show her support, give me a kick in the ass, and try to distract me from my dark mood.

After sliding out of bed, I padded across the cabin toward the door. It had started raining a few hours ago, and it sounded like a sad song playing on my roof, echoing into the dark space.

When I pulled the door open, I knew my eyes were deceiving me. Or my mind was. The woman I thought I saw standing in front of me could not be the one who was really there. I just stood there for a moment, my chest moving as I stared at the woman who had been the creator of every high in my life, and the reason for every low.

"Matt . . ."

When she said my name, I knew I wasn't seeing things or imagining her. Her hair and bathrobe were wet from the rain, her skin gleaming and prickled with goose bumps. Her light eyes lit up the dark, looking as though they'd been through their own storm tonight.

She was here. In front of me. Inches away.

It was the scenario I'd always hoped for, but it was for a different reason than the one I needed. She was here to make sure I was all right. I'd tell her I was of course, then she'd walk away, back to him, and nothing would be all right.

"What do you want, Cora?" My hands curled into the doorway above my head. I needed support. I wasn't sure I could keep standing on my own two feet any longer. "I'm tired—exhausted. You and me." My head shook slowly. "I can't keep doing this."

She slid a step closer. Then another. Her eyes ran up my body until they finished on mine. There was a look in them I'd never seen before, one I didn't have a name for. All I knew was that looking at her looking at me gave me a current of hope where none had been.

Her hands spread over my stomach, and her fingers curled into me. Her touch felt like a shockwave reverberating through me until I felt nothing else.

"Neither can I," she whispered, moving closer again so her body was pressed against the length of mine.

Her words hadn't finished forming before her mouth crashed into mine. I was so surprised by it, I staggered back, and she fell back with me. Forming my arms around her, I regained my footing long enough to kick the door closed before I backed her into the room.

This could have been a dream. This could have been reality. It didn't matter. What mattered was that I was there with her now. I wasn't going to waste a moment second-guessing or punching pause to consider if this was right or wrong.

Her arms tied around my neck as I lifted her, my own arms winding around her body like I was trying to find the best hold. As though I were trying to figure out a way to hold on to her without ever letting go.

Her lips moved against mine in feverish, random pulses until I couldn't breathe. As I lowered her onto the bed, I pulled back just enough so I could look her in the eyes. She stared right back, no measure of doubt or guilt consuming them.

"Tell me you're here because you want to be with me." I crawled up the bed with her in my arms, feeling the wet from her clothes seep into mine, feeling her chest move hard against mine from the way we were both breathing. "Tell me you're here because you want me."

When Cora's head was settled into a pillow, I leaned back so I was hovering above her, knees pinned over her lap, eyes aimed at the single most perfect sight I'd ever seen. Her in my bed, having chosen me, staring at me like I was the only one who could give her what she needed.

Her hand found mine, and her palm pressed into mine before she braided our fingers together. The ring was gone. The engagement ring, the wedding band—they were both gone.

"I'm here because I want to be with you." Her other hand slid my hair back from my forehead. "I want you, Matt."

When I exhaled, I felt purged. All at once. Instantly. From all of the false hopes and pain, the secret longing and ache.

Cora worked my shirt up my body, furious and fast. Once she'd pulled it off her hands moved over me in the same fashion. My chest crashed back down over hers, the ache between my legs so intense I felt as if I could blackout. When I pivoted my hips into hers, the ache receded just enough for my vision to clear. Cora gasped, pumping her hips into mine again, her cold, wet legs twisting around my back.

My mouth found hers. Our tongues collided together as though we were racing against time, the end of the world moments away.

The way her breath caught when my hands touched her in certain places.

The way she gasped when I pressed my lap into hers.

The sound of her exhale, ragged and drawn-out, when my mouth moved against her neck.

Those sounds I'd never forget. No matter where life went from this moment, they'd stay a part of me forever. The sounds Cora made for me as I loved her body was enough to sustain a man in his darkest hour on his darkest day.

When her hands slipped between us, her fingers working madly to undo my jeans before tearing them off, my body stilled.

"Wait," I breathed against her neck. "Slow down. Let me take my time with you." When my lips covered her neck this time, they crept slowly across her skin, tasting the way the rain mixed with the salt of her skin. My hand slid up the bends of her body, memorizing every dip and curve. She shuddered below me, her own body stilling. "My whole life has been stolen moments, closed doors, and rushed encounters with you. I don't want to rush right now. Let me just enjoy you. Let me just *be* with you."

When I came to the place where I'd left my mark on her, I touched it. This would fade until one day, there'd be no trace of the mark I'd left on her. Could it be that I'd left a different kind of mark behind though? One that wasn't so temporal? Was that the reason she was here? Because my mark on her was more than skin-deep?

Cora moved beneath me, lifting off her back to slip out of her robe. I found the tie and unknotted it slowly, letting myself memorize the feel of the material rubbing against the pads of my fingers, the strength of the knot, working against it for what felt like forever until, suddenly, it seemed to come undone all at once.

I slid the robe off of her shoulders, down her arms, off her hands, never allowing my eyes to look anywhere but into hers. A beautiful as she was, as spread out below me in a little cover-up as she was, I'd always known where that beauty originated from, its hidden source—her eyes.

My hand curved around her cheek, the other winding behind her back, and I pressed myself into her, lowering her back to the bed. This time when our mouths met, they moved slowly, as though time was an infinite entity and life was nothing beyond this moment.

"Matt," she whispered against my lips, her fingers trailing down the canyon of my back.

Hearing her say my name, having her in my arms when she said it, made something low and uneven vibrate in my chest. Her mouth came around to my ear, where the sound of her shallow, uneven breaths ignited something inside me I wasn't sure I could ever extinguish. When she whispered my name again, this time right beside my ear, I pressed myself between her legs, feeling dizzy from the thought of her saying my name like that when I was moving inside her.

When her hips lifted up to meet mine the next time I ground against her, I grabbed a fistful of her nightgown and pulled it up around her stomach. I didn't stop rocking against her, my mouth claiming hers once more, as I made love to her, half-dressed, my body not yet entering hers.

I could tell from the way she was breathing that she was close. From the way she was twisting in my arms, her nails digging into my skin. I was just as close, feeling my own release rising from inside.

"Please, Matt," she breathed.

My jaw ground to keep me from losing it the moment her hand gripped me, stroking me in a way that had me close to blacking out again. What was I doing? Why was I stalling? What had I needed to tell her before we did this again?

The reminder found its way into my consciousness, but just as it rose from my chest, another voice settled into the air around us.

"Hey, Matt!" The sound of feet moving quickly up the stairs outside. "We need to talk!"

The sound of a door being opened

The sound of silence, the kind more deafening than a sonic boom.

The sound of my brother's sharp inhale as his eyes adjusted to the darkness.

Those were the sounds I'd also remember from tonight. The ones that would follow me to the grave, along with the others.

"What the fuck?" His words came out in a rush of air.

Lifting off of Cora, my eyes found hers and held there for a moment. In them, I tried to tell her it would be okay, that I'd take care of this. But her face was frozen in shock, her eyes filling with guilt, as she scrambled out from beneath me, adjusting her cover-up and pulling at the sheets to cover herself.

"How could you?" Jacob's voice was quiet, quivering.

His eyes connected with mine once I turned to face him. Everything I expected to find was there on his face: betrayal, shock, outrage . . . even a shadow of sadness.

"You son of a bitch. I knew it. I knew you wouldn't waste your chance to slide into my spot." His volume grew with every word, his eyes becoming feral. "I can't believe you." Jacob's eyes shifted over my shoulder.

Instinctively, I slid into his view.

"I can't believe you," he spat again, thrusting his arms back at where Cora had retreated up against the headboard.

"Jacob, I'm sorry." Her voice caught as though she was guilty of this whole mess. To blame for everything that had gone wrong in the course of our twenty years together. "I never meant for you to find out this way. I should have come to you first. I should have explained—"

"Explained what?" Jacob shouted, sweeping a couple of glasses from the table with his arm. They crashed to the floor and shattered. "That you'd had enough of me? That you wanted to move on to the other brother? Just to see if you were missing out on anything? Just to see if he could give you something I couldn't?" The vein running down Jacob's forehead was bursting through the skin, his body quaking from the emotions coursing through him. "Just to see if he could make you scream his name louder when you opened your legs for him?"

"Jacob!" I slid off the bed, keeping myself between him and Cora as I approached, my hands raised. "This is more than just some endless battle between us for her. This is more than one of us coming out the winner and the other the loser." Every step I took toward him, he took one toward me. "This is more than that. This is more."

When I stopped moving, he did too. A few feet separated us, but from the betrayal on his face, I knew that while physical space might be one thing, after tonight, an impossible distance would be between us going forward. Unlike me, he wouldn't be content to wait on the sidelines for years on end while another man loved the woman he did. He wouldn't be content to do right by her no matter what, even if that meant letting someone else take the credit for his efforts.

"Yeah, no shit this is more." His eyes dropped, narrowing when they fell on my open fly. "This is my brother, my best friend, fucking the woman who was supposed to be my wife behind my back. On our own damn honeymoon."

"This isn't our honeymoon." Cora's voice came from behind me. "You never showed up for the wedding to make this a honeymoon."

Jacob's eyes latched onto her. "We've been over this a million times already. I don't know what happened. I don't remember." He started pacing, rolling his neck. "For all I know, you could have been behind it. Drugging me so you could sneak off with this guy and finally get him out of your system."

"Jacob, stop," I ordered, trying to keep my voice and body calm. It was challenging, especially with the way he was the total opposite.

"I've never been looking for ways to get Matt out of my system," Cora said slowly. "I don't want him out of my system."

I was expecting it, so I was able to block him before he got a step toward her. "Step back, Jacob," I ordered, but he didn't listen. Not that I was expecting him to.

Now that we were closer, I could smell it. The liquor. He'd been drinking. Not enough to be stumbling, slurring drunk, but enough to lower his inhibitions and make him more dangerous.

"You step back, you traitorous bastard." Jacob shoved me, but I didn't budge. "That's my girl. My fiancée. Not yours." His finger stabbed the air in Cora's direction.

"She's not something to possess."

He rolled his head to the side, cracking his neck. "No? Because you seem to be under the impression you can just take her without asking permission."

"He didn't take me." From the sound of movement, I guessed Cora was climbing off the bed. I wasn't going to look back to confirm it though; I didn't dare take my eyes off of Jacob for one second in his current condition. "This was my choice. My decision. I'm here with him because I want to be, not because he took anything."

For the briefest moment, sadness settled into his eyes. It was unmistakable, raw, and fleeting. This wasn't the way I'd wanted things to happen. This wasn't how I'd wanted him to find out. Despite my brother's downfalls and mistakes, he deserved better than this.

I was a knot of emotions, a dozen different agendas pulling me in different directions. Protecting her, protecting him, wanting to explain, wanting to go back in time, looking for the rights words to say that could fix all of this.

This couldn't be fixed though. The damage had been done. All I could do was try to protect them both.

"Jacob, I'm sorry. This wasn't what I planned. We'd never want to hurt you, but she's made her choice." I moved with him as his paces went wider. "Can you try to respect that?"

Jacob stopped, turning so we were facing each other, his eyes unrecognizable. "Can I try to respect that? Sure, I guess I can try to respect that." He paused for a minute, his eyes lifting like he was considering it right then. "Sorry, not going to work for me."

I caught a glimpse of it in his eye before his body went into motion, but not in time to move. Just enough time to brace myself for it.

Jacob's fist came around fast, and right on target. When it cracked me in the jaw, all I concentrated on was staying on my feet and not retaliating. This wasn't the first fist I'd taken from my brother, but it was the first one I'd taken without paying it back. Part of me took it because I knew I deserved it. Another part realized getting into a fight with my brother wouldn't solve a damn thing.

So I let him have a free one.

Cora gave a little cry. I heard the sound of her feet rushing closer, but I lifted my arm at her, shaking my head.

"How's that for respect, brother? Not that a piece of shit like you would know anything about it." Jacob shook his fist, bouncing like he was just getting warmed up.

Moving my jaw around, I positioned myself directly in front of him. "Respect it or don't, but she's made her choice."

His arm moved so fast this time, I didn't have time to brace for the hit. The sound of his knuckles connecting with my jaw pierced the air, the sound of Cora's shouts echoing with it.

I staggered to the side a few steps, but I didn't go down. I couldn't. If Jacob needed to use me as a human punching bag to diffuse his anger, fine. If he was so exhausted at the end of beating the shit out of me that he didn't have any energy left to target at her, that worked just fine for me.

"Jacob, stop!" Cora came up behind me, her hands dropping to my shoulders as she pulled on me like she was trying to yank me away from him. "This is your brother for god's sake. Enough."

"That's right. He is my brother. You'd think that came with some kind of loyalty, wouldn't you?" Jacob was shaking out his fist again. A couple of his knuckles were bleeding. Or maybe that was my blood. I could taste it in my mouth and feel it trickling down from my lip. "Then again, you're my fiancée and I just found you beneath another man, so maybe loyalty's gone extinct."

"You are the last person to be talking about loyalty," Cora snapped.

"And the last person I'm going to take morality lessons from is a two-timing whore."

Breaking out of Cora's hold, I stormed toward him, shoving him so hard he fell back into the wall. My arms were trembling at my sides, my fists curling, begging to be put to use.

All that did was make him laugh. Like we were all in on some joke and had just discovered so. Lifting his arms out at his sides, Jacob stopped when he was a few steps in front of me. "This is your chance, Matt. Your chance to get me back." He turned his head so his cheek was facing me, his arms still raised like he was offering himself to me. "To take it out on me for all the times I know you wanted to. For all the times it was my arms she went into instead of yours. All the times she picked me over you. All the times you heard her sighs coming from behind my bedroom door. This is your chance to beat the shit out of me like you wanted to do all of those times."

My body was trembling. From wanting to let him have it, from trying to hold back. I felt like so much adrenaline was filling my body, it was seeping out of my pores.

"You're wrong." I closed the distance between us by a step. "I didn't want to beat the shit out of you back then."

He huffed. "You hated me for it. You hated me because I had her and you didn't."

My head shook slowly, and I held my hands up like I was making a truce. "I didn't hate you. I *loved* her."

So much for my truce. It wasn't Jacob's fist that came at me then—it was his whole body. Barreling in my direction, he drove me into the wall on the other side of the room. The breath rushed out of my lungs from the impact right before he drove his fists into me like he couldn't land them fast enough.

Cora rushed up behind us, looking like she was about to get in the mix and try to tear us apart. The thought of her coming between us when Jacob was like this shot panic into my bloodstream.

"Cora, no." My head shook when my eyes found hers. It was enough to stop her, though I knew it wouldn't last for long.

Jacob's hits continued to pummel my stomach until I felt myself about to double over. Twisting, I managed to get my shoulder into him, and I lunged forward, driving him across the room until we rammed into a table. A lamp tumbled over the side, breaking when it hit the floor, but neither of us acknowledged it. We were in a different world.

Now my fists were flying, connecting wherever they could. Jacob grinned up at me as I continued to land hit after hit, like he was enjoying this.

"See? Doesn't that feel better?" Jacob laughed right before kicking my feet out beneath me.

I hit the floor hard, making the pictures on the walls shake. He was on me instantly, pinning my arms and delivering hit after hit, his aim on my face. I didn't know where the surge of strength came from, but the next moment, I was back on top of him, swinging at him while he swung at me. Our knees, elbows, and fists were a blur of motion.

I'd never felt this way before. This kind of rage. The kind that made everything in my vision glow red. I'd never realized I was capable of the power I possessed or what it was capable of doing. I felt it all bubble to the surface right then. All of the times I'd suppressed my feelings, every time I'd buried them deep, they all burst free at the same time, fueling my anger and my fists.

The fight felt like it would never come to an end. It was clear neither of us would be the first to tap out, and even though we'd been at it for a while, neither of our strikes were dimming in power or enthusiasm.

"That's enough! Both of you!" Cora had been silent in the corner for long enough. She came charging forward. "You're both going to kill each other."

She grabbed my arm, pulling it back before it could connect with Jacob. That left one side of me vulnerable, and Jacob didn't waste a moment. The instant he hit me, I went flying back, but I wasn't the only one. With the way Cora was still holding on to me, she staggered back and tripped over one of Jacob's shoes that had come off during the brawl. She hit the ground hard, the back of her head ramming into the table behind her.

The sound it made when she hit it was the most disturbing noise I'd heard yet.

Jacob and I went instantly still, both of our heads turning toward where she'd fallen. I crawled toward her, my vision blurred from what I guessed was a black eye or two starting to form. Jacob rolled onto his side, heaving for a breath, trying to make his way toward her too.

"Don't. Just don't." Cora's hand moved behind her head, rubbing it.

I stilled, not sure what to do. I wanted to go to her, but from the look on her face, that was not what she wanted.

"Look at you two. You're brothers. Twin brothers." She sat up, motioning between Jacob and me bloodied and broken on the floor. "You're fighting over a girl. Over me. I won't come between you." Her head shook as she started to stand. She wobbled a few times, but she shook her head when I moved to help. "I refuse to be the reason you two rip each other apart. We've been through too damn much for that."

She didn't know, or she hadn't accepted, that she'd been what had come between us for years. This was nothing new. This was just all of those years coming to a head. A bloody, brutal one.

Her eyes filled with tears when they met mine, but she didn't let a single one fall. "I can't do this."

When she headed toward the door, I moved to stand. "Cora—"

She didn't stop, didn't look back. I didn't even know if she heard me. She was leaving, and I understood why. She loved us both. In different ways maybe, but she cared about us and couldn't stand to be the reason we killed each other, literally or figuratively.

She was moving through the door when Jacob's throat cleared. "I was with someone else." He didn't sound anything like the person he'd been minutes ago. He sounded like the brother I remembered, the one I loved and respected. "That's why I didn't make it to the wedding. I went out, met someone, got drunk, and let her take me home."

Cora turned slowly in the doorway.

"I made a mistake. I've made lots of mistakes, Cora." He sighed as his confession continued, his eyes never wandering from hers. "I never wanted to hurt you. I loved you, but I'm a self-destructive, greedy son of a bitch. I'm sorry."

She didn't say anything. She stood there framed in the doorway, the rain coming down behind her. Instead of a look of despair covering her face, she looked more peaceful than anything else. "Thank you for being honest," she whispered, stepping back onto the porch. "Good-bye, Jacob."

She didn't say anything else. She just turned into the night and rushed down the porch into the rain.

"Cora!" I called, pushing myself to a stand. It took more effort than it should have, but that might have been because every bone in my body felt either broken or bruised. Same for every muscle.

She didn't stop, and a few moments later, the dark swallowed her.

"Cora!" I tried again. My first few motions forward were more a hobble than a step.

"Going to need to move faster than that if you're going to catch her." Jacob had scooted back into a wall, wiping his face off with his shirt. It came away with streaks of blood and sweat.

"You look like shit," I said, realizing what part of my motion was so damn slow. I'd been barefoot when I charged over a mess of broken glass.

"Yeah, well, I feel like shit, so at least the outside matches the inside for once in my life."

I limped a few more steps toward the door, each one feeling easier than the last, despite the shooting pain from whatever glass fragments I'd managed to imbed into the bottoms of my feet.

I wanted to go after her. I needed to, but when I looked at my brother collapsed into the corner, I couldn't just leave. Not yet. Making my way over to him, I held my hand out to give him a pull up.

He shook his head. "I can't move. I'd just fall back down if I did make it up." Jacob opened his mouth, moving his jaw from side to side to see if it was still working. "When did you learn to kick ass like that, by the way?"

My shoulder lifted. Which also hurt like hell. "It came naturally."

Jacob chuckled a few beats, wincing when he shifted. Probably because he had a few cracked ribs like I did.

"That's going to need stitches," I said, indicating his left brow where a stream of blood was running from a nice gash.

"Good thing my brother's a doctor." His sliver of a smile revealed teeth tinged red with blood.

"I'm sorry. I really am."

Before I could say more, he lifted his hand. "I know."

We didn't say anything after that, and I wasn't sure if there was anything left to be said.

When I moved for the door again, something landed at my feet.

"Put on some fucking pants. You're going after the girl. You got the girl," Jacob said, the look on his face telling that the words left a sour taste in his mouth. "Don't show up in your underwear for Christ's sake."

I found myself smiling as I pulled on my jeans, not that I knew why. My relationship with my brother would forever be strained because of this night. I wasn't sure if we could have much, if any, relationship from here. My relationship with Cora was . . . a question mark. Twenty minutes ago I'd known, but now, I wasn't sure. She hadn't seen the best side of me just now, and I couldn't blame her for having second thoughts about wanting to be with me after everything.

After everything we'd been through, nothing could go back to being the same.

I knew that, and I was willing to pay that price to have her in my life. I wasn't sure if she felt the same.

"Maybe I really do love her the real way, after all." Jacob's voice cut through the quiet as I moved through the door.

I was at a loss for how to respond to that. "Yeah?"

He was staring at his hands, turning them over like he was trying to remember them. "I'm letting her go so she can be with the one of us who can love her the way she deserves."

CHAPTER EIGHTEEN

Cora

My mom used to tell me that nothing worth having in life came easy. Or cheap.

I'd never realized how true those words were until now. This hadn't come easy. It felt like it had cost me almost everything I had to give. But I knew he was worth having.

I knew he'd been worth the hard work, worth the fight, worth the cost.

Matt Adams was worth it all.

The journey that had led me to this realization had taken years, and the price of accepting it had been dear. Three lives had been uprooted by it. Three lives had been permanently affected by me realizing what I'd really known all along—I might have wanted them both in my life, but there was only one I couldn't live without.

The rain had finished the job of drenching me a while ago as I stood on the beach, having a heart-to-heart with the dark ocean. It was funny how a silent conversation with an inanimate object could reveal so much. I guessed silence was sometimes the only way to hear what your heart had been trying to tell you all along.

The beach was empty—the late hour and a torrential downpour had a way of doing that—but I couldn't imagine being anywhere else. I was right where I needed to be. The answers I'd been chasing for the past few days had been right here, waiting for me to accept them.

I finally had.

It was the same beach Matt and I had snorkeled from, and I found myself smiling at the memory of him emerging from that mobile changing room, trying to be the picture of confidence as he strutted into the water in a patch of python-print fabric. All of my memories of Matt were like that—drawing smiles when reflected upon. It had been obvious, so obvious, but I'd been so very blind.

Because of it, I'd hurt them both. I'd do anything I could to make it up to them, but I guessed only one would allow me to. The other was lost to me in all ways. Jacob was the price I'd paid for Matt, and it seemed unfair that one had cost me the other.

The rain was coming down like every cloud up there had just opened up, and it was so dark, I was lucky to see what was a few feet in front of me, but I knew the moment he found me. I felt the moment he saw me. He was as much a part of me as I was a part of him, our bond breaking through the metaphysical.

"Come on. Let's get you out of the storm." Matt's voice surrounded me before I could see him.

A few moments later, he came into view. He was walking funny and he was barely recognizable. One eye was sealed shut, the other swollen, his bottom lip busted open as a mix of blood and rain trickled from it. He was still shirtless, but he'd pulled on his jeans. I'd never seen him like this, but as he kept coming closer, his hand reaching out for me, I knew he'd never been so perfect in my eyes. He'd come for me, he'd found me, he'd waited for me . . . he'd saved me.

"Why? I'm not afraid of the storm. It can't touch me." I angled toward him, lifting my hand to capture his. "You've always been my shelter from the storm. You've been my stronghold keeping me safe from the rest of the world even when I didn't know it was you. Your walls might have been invisible, but they were invincible."

Matt swallowed, hobbling one last step closer. "Maggie."

I nodded. "Maggie."

When his arm lifted so he could slide my wet hair over my shoulder, he winced but didn't stop. "What did she tell you?"

My arm looped around his waist gently as I stared up at him. Bloody. Broken. Bruised. He was so damn beautiful it hurt. "Everything."

Matt didn't say anything. He just stood there, his fingers combing through my hair, seeming to melt into the bend of my arm around him.

"Why didn't you tell me?" I asked.

The skin between his brows creased. "Because it didn't matter who saved you that night, just that you were okay. I didn't care who you thought was making you happy, just that you were."

I didn't know I'd been hollow until his words filled every empty space and dark corner inside me.

His hand molded behind my neck, his thumb brushing along my hairline and tracing the bandage covering my cut. "How can you forgive me? How can you ever trust me again after what I did?"

It took me a moment to realize what he was talking about. All I could think about was all of the ways he'd earned my trust, everything he'd done for me, selflessly and endlessly.

"You made a split-second decision at the wedding, Matt. I can't blame you for that. You were trying to do the right thing."

His head shook, sending rain falling like diamonds from the ends of his hair. "Not the wedding day."

My other hand lifted to his face. "You were drinking. We both were. We've been over this."

"I might have had a few drinks, but when I leaned in, when I put my hands on you and drew you to me, that wasn't the alcohol. That was me. All me." His forehead creased. "You trusted me, and I betrayed that trust."

When I blinked at him, rain spilled from my lashes. "I knew it was you." I had to say it again. Louder. "I knew it was you, Matt." I paused to make sure he'd heard me. To make sure he understood what I was saying. "I might have been afraid to admit it to myself, but I knew. Deep inside, I knew it."

He watched me for a minute, searching my face for any signs of doubt. He wouldn't find any. His arm slid behind my neck as he pulled me to him and stiffly wound his other arm behind my back. He turned us slightly so the rain was pelting his back instead of mine. We stood like that for a while, our toes in the wet sand, our bodies pressed together, our arms clinging to each other.

"I need to tell you something." My head lifted from his chest so I could look up at him. "Something I've been waiting to say for twenty years."

He shook his head, a smile starting to form. "Me first."

Not a chance.

"I love you," I blurted, so loud and fast it surprised him.

That look of surprise was chased away by something else. Another emotion that made my heart stop. "Again," he whispered.

I lifted onto my toes so I was closer to his eye level. "I love you." I pressed my lips to his.

His eyes were still closed from our kiss, his hands drawing me closer. "Again."

I leaned in, dropping my mouth outside of his ear. "I love you."

His chest moved against mine, our breaths coming into sync. "Don't stop saying that. Ever."

My eyebrow lifted when he opened his eyes. "That might present a challenge."

"One I'm sure you'll find a way to overcome." He winked, his fingers brushing across the seam of my lips. "Those words, coming from your mouth, when your eyes are on mine, that's the reason. Right there, those three words, that's the answer."

My head tipped as I gently touched his swollen lip. "The answer to what?"

He stared at me like it should have been obvious. "My question for existence. My reason for living. My explanation for twenty years of waiting."

"Oh yeah. That little reason."

He prodded at my sides, making me laugh. When I squirmed against him, he just picked me up, tying my legs behind him.

"You're broken. Everywhere," I added when he grimaced after adjusting his footing. "You need a doctor—one other than yourself—and a good night of sleep before you start tossing me around."

"First things first."

"Pain meds, then doctor?" I guessed, fastening my hands above his shoulders.

He sighed, then his face got serious. Really serious. My throat instantly went dry.

"I know this might seem like I'm rushing things, but I've been waiting two decades to ask you this question." He didn't pause, didn't clear his throat, didn't look away. He didn't um and er and stall the hell out of it. There was only confidence in his voice, matching the look on his face.

"Matt," I whispered, not sure anymore if the drops running down my face were rain.

"I'm going to keep it simple and sweet because if you haven't figured out why I'm asking you this question, I haven't done my job." He tipped his head back up at me, his eyes waiting for mine. The moment my eyes met his, he smiled. "Will you marry me?"

Definitely not raindrops. Nope. At least not all of them. My hands moved from his shoulders to his face as I lowered my face above his. "Technically, I already married you."

He chuckled, shaking his head. "Will you marry me again? This time with my name on the actual marriage certificate?"

My lips met his. Then again. He tasted like sweat and rain and even a bit of blood. He tasted like the fight of my life. The fight I'd won. "Yes."

"Are you sure?" He started to spin slow circles on the beach, grinning at me like he had so many times before—like I was his reason. His answer. "It's a big commitment, a lifelong one from what I've heard. Don't you want to take a few minutes to think about it?"

My hand found his left hand and knitted our fingers together while he managed to hold me with one arm. He'd taken off his ring like I had. We'd both let go of what was keeping us apart so we could hold on to what had kept us together. Each other.

"I don't need another minute to think," I said. "I've been waiting twenty years to give you your answer."

"That answer being?" He turned his ear toward me, waiting.

"No. Absolutely not." I managed to keep a straight face right up until Matt turned his mock-wounded face toward me. "Yes. The answer is yes. The answer is always yes."

He kissed me again, this one not coming to a foreseeable end. He stood there in the rain, holding me while we kissed until both of us were gasping for breath. The moment I sucked in a deep breath, I wanted to kiss him all over again.

"Can you believe this is how it went?" he asked, his chest moving fast against mine. "What it took for us to be together?"

I thought about that for a moment. Condensing the countless years we'd spent together into a few moments, I thought about everything we'd been through to get us to this perfect moment in time. After all that, I'd believe anything. After all this, I knew anything was possible.

"I married the wrong brother," I said, dropping my forehead to his. Matt was the one. He always had been. He always would be. He was my Mister Right. "But he turned out to be the right one."

The End

Thank you for reading MISTER WRONG
by NEW YORK TIMES and USATODAY
bestselling author, Nicole Williams.

Nicole loves to hear from her readers.
You can connect with her on:

Facebook: Nicole Williams (Official Author Page)
Twitter: nwilliamsbooks
Blog: nicoleawilliams.blogspot.com

Other Works by Nicole:

HATE STORY

CRASH, CLASH, and CRUSH (HarperCollins)

UP IN FLAMES (Simon & Schuster UK)

LOST & FOUND, NEAR & FAR, HEART & SOUL

FINDERS KEEPERS, LOSERS WEEPERS

STEALING HOME, TOUCHING DOWN

COLLARED

THE FABLE OF US

THREE BROTHERS

HARD KNOX, DAMAGED GOODS

CROSSING STARS

GREAT EXPLOITATIONS

THE EDEN TRILOGY

THE PATRICK CHRONICLES

Made in the USA
San Bernardino, CA
10 March 2017